Forbidden Encounters

Date: October 27, 2019

Lanae Gee

authorHOUSE

AuthorHouse™
1663 Liberty Drive
Bloomington, IN 47403
www.authorhouse.com
Phone: 1 (800) 839-8640

Published by AuthorHouse 11/19/2019

ISBN: 978-1-7283-3581-0 (sc)
ISBN: 978-1-7283-3580-3 (e)

Print information available on the last page.

Any people depicted in stock imagery provided by Getty Images are models, and such images are being used for illustrative purposes only. Certain stock imagery © Getty Images.

This book is printed on acid-free paper.

Because of the dynamic nature of the Internet, any web addresses or links contained in this book may have changed since publication and may no longer be valid. The views expressed in this work are solely those of the author and do not necessarily reflect the views of the publisher, and the publisher hereby disclaims any responsibility for them.

This is a work of fiction. All of the characters, names, incidents, organizations, and dialogue in this novel are either the products of the author's imagination or are used fictitiously.

Dedication

To My Future *NXavier*

She is not perfect!
She is Sensual but Opinionated,
She is Confident and Alluring,
She is Self-reliant, not Self-centered,
She Resilient, but Empathetic,
She is independent but would rather be swept off
her feet by her knight in shining armor.
She is a charming romantic but is level headed.
She is multifaceted, and a work in progress, so be gentle with her heart.
She is not easy to understand or love, but she loves unconditionally.
You must be strong enough to handle her, be mature, and experienced
to sufficiently mold her into the delicate flower that she is.
Be patient with her, or you may never be introduced
to the Enigma that she was involved in.
Finally, remember to love her for who she is!
She cannot promise you that she will never annoy you, she will…
But you will never have to wonder if she loves you!
Lanae G

Acknowledgment

I could certainly not say thank you enough to **Kiara**, my Mia, my best friend who has worked as diligently as I have on this book, thanks for your keen interest, perseverance, and encouragement. She assisted greatly with the most intricate details as an editor, a supporter, and a true friend. This book is as much mine as it is yours. I love you!

To **Mathe**, my Lorelai, my other best friend, who assisted in many ways to keep me grounded. Thanks for your love and support.

To **Sharms**, a long-ago friend who resurfaced at the right time, this book would not have been possible without your criticism, your opinions, your belief in me, and your encouragement.

To **Joana, Veronique, Veronica, Alvin,** and **TB,** thanks for believing in me and encouraging me when I did not think I had it in me.

To my family, I know this was another reason why I avoided all family activities, please understand that I am grateful and thankful for managing without me.

I am infinitely grateful for your guidance, love, encouragement, and tireless support. I love all of you and would like to express my sincerest gratitude for your continued belief in me. I am blessed to have such a distinguished group of family and friends.

Thanks for making my dreams come true and always being there for me.

Lanae G

Her Constant

☆☆☆☆☆☆☆☆☆☆☆☆☆☆☆☆☆

She was naked, naked, and floating...
Floating for eternity, searching and calling his name
Suddenly he appears, he always does…
She is now naked and floating, floating to his waiting arms...
They were still there waiting for her, they are always there
She felt the warm water on her skin and the cool
breeze blowing all around her naked body.
She knew that he would keep her warm, all the stress and anxiety
of previous weeks melted away from her naked body, she floated
closer, her bare skin felt more heated the closer she got to him.
She swam to his open arms, her body aching to be in his arms
She felt the warmth of his body as he wrapped
his strong arms around her.
Her Heart rate increased fervently, she collapsed into his arms
His soothing voice calmed her thunderous
heartbeats, he pulled her to him
She was naked because only in her nakedness
she can feel his need for her,

She needed him as he needed her, she rested her cheeks
on his heart and felt the sudden rise and fall of his chest,
and she can feel his warm breath on her face.
His thighs support hers as she lay floating in his arms.
He is her constant...
He is her always
He is her fortress...
He is her heart...
He makes her smile
He has the power to break her because she
is so vulnerable in his arms.
She is only vulnerable to him; he can cripple her with mere words
He brings out the best and worst in her;
she remains naked in his arms.
He is home!!
She was naked!
Yet she was floating, floating on blue water;
he is her wings over water
She kept her eyes closed to picture him, his rare smiles, his
dry sense of humor, his quirks, his power over her.
He is the key
He has eyes that could see right through her as she
lays naked in his arms, he makes her smile.
The warmth of his naked skin makes her blush...
He has awakened feelings that she thought were lost forever.
He has magical powers, how did he do it?
How did he discard her fears?
How did he get her in the water floating and naked?
She needs him; she wants to be naked in his
strong arms against his hard chest.
She feels comforted...
She feels safe...
She belongs there
He has cast a spell on her aching heart, and
her fragile heartaches to follow him...
Follow him anywhere, throwing caution to the wind, at all cost.

x

Follow him to the clouds...follow him to the stars...
Following his naked body to the ends of
creation, oh, how heartaches too.
She remains naked, floating and naked,
naked for his brown eyes only.
Naked and afraid that he lets her go; afraid that would ever go away
He laid right next to her and watch her
naked body locked in his embrace.
She felt him shudder, she knows that he is overwhelmed.
Overwhelmed by her smooth naked skin so warm in his arms.
She remained in his arms as the water floats around him.
Is he cold??
Is he comfortable?
She needs to know; she asked, he denied!
She wrapped her arms around his shoulders,
and her arms massage his back anyway.
She loves his smooth skin; she loves being so close to him.
She belongs to him; he is her King, her Savior
She can only get that close to him in her purest state.
She was naked and floating on the blue waters, floating naked
while the waves gently rocked her body from side to side.
She felt at peace, she had not felt so at peace in ages
She welcomes the glimpse of moonlight covering his naked body.
He cradles her naked body closer to him...
Her mind drifted to him as it does so often lately.
He is her light
He is her purpose...
He is her pleasure...
He is her pain.
He fills her mind on days when there is no need for his presence.
He centers her, he keeps her grounded; she hates that her day is
controlled by his interactions; he dominates her subconscious.
She laid naked next to him as he silently stared at the
stars above them, his fingers intertwine with hers.
She never wants to be away from him, It's
too hard. He could feel her...

He drew her closer to his chest and brought her wet
fingers to his lips. Then he lowered his lips to hers.
Only at this very point, she realized
She was his constant.
She was his always.
He holds her nakedness, as she holds his naked body
As she felt his breath, …and his lips devoured hers, she closed
her eyes and thought of his constant presence in her mind…
She loves him there
She wants him forever

Lanae Gee

Introduction

HOPEFUL BEGINNINGS

Orianthi Page laid in bed blankly staring at the television but seeing nothing. Tonight, she was extremely distracted, too bored to read Lisa Kleypas' book laying on her chest, constantly rewinding the shows the was watching, also drained to enjoy it.

Something was missing, something felt off. Orianthi craved a specific human interaction, not in the form of her girlfriends, which she spoke to on her way home from work. No, she missed having an adult, male companion. Someone to whisper sweet nothings to her.

Fantasizing about being with someone lacks the real flair of having a conversation with someone you love. She misses discussing her day with someone. She misses cuddling with that special someone, to rest on his chest, synchronizing their heartbeats, and falling asleep in his arms. She needed that. Orianthi looked around her bed at her many pillows, her laptop, and her books around her and wished that they were temporary, but this is her norm. She was very lonesome and needed a hiatus from this loneliness. Yes, she required physical contact; her daydreams were no longer sufficient to sustain her.

She craves fulfillment, she needed love, she needed the sensation of human touch. She was drowning tonight in a sea of loneliness. She needed to find someone to fill this empty void in her, she needed to date, and she definitely needed to fall in love again. It was two years since her divorce, and she was finally over the guilt of running away when it fell apart. She was relieved to be moving on from this stressful chapter of her life. Orianthi was not ready for another relationship, but available to date and meet someone interesting. She assessed all the possible male prospects in her life, and they all failed to meet her criteria. All her other potential possibilities were black men, Caribbean born, similar experiences, so she needed a new adventure, with a different storyline. She always secretly envisioned the thought of dating a Caucasian male, a secret fetish that she had only shared with her two best friends. At this point in her life, Orianthi would like to explore this fetish. Before she loses her nerve, she found herself downloading the app on her phone and signing onto an interracial dating site.

She was apprehensive at first, but within days had quite a few suitors. She expected to just explore this new fetish of hers for a while and did not expect to see 'him' so soon. She was scanning through the list of "who favored her" when she came across his profile. He was handsome. He was 5 years her senior, 6 feet 2 inches to her 5 feet, 2 inches. He had thick, curly, wavy jet black hair that one can get loss combing their fingers through. He had piercing green eyes, broad, muscular shoulders, lean chest, well-chiseled arms that show he was capable of lifting anything. His abdomen appeared flat and well defined under his Ralph Lauren polo shirt. His hips seem svelte in his jeans, and she was able to identify a considerable bulge in the front. His thighs appeared muscular and firm under his jeans, he was breathtakingly appealing. She continues to scan his photos and profile details, he had a post-graduate degree, progressive in his political views, his smile was captivatingly displaying his white teeth, she liked his smile. She was quite happy he was a nonsmoker, he was a father, the stranger drank socially, and his profile boasts of a retired naval officer, but he was now an engineer. She was enthralled.

She had seen all 15 seasons of NCIS 3 times. So she was more fascinated with the fact that he was a retired Naval officer than his engineering portfolio. In his profile, he wrote that he loved the indoors and loved being at home, which was honest and appealing to her. She rarely gets out of her home on an occasional day off. So he sounded like her ideal prospect in every line of his profile. She was intrigued! She blushed at the thought of those strong arms wrapped around her body, being pulled to his chest, he lifted her chin to look into his face or feeling his thick lips on hers. She could hardly wait to talk to him. She knew that her thoughts of this total stranger were both puzzling and pre-mature, but she couldn't prevent herself from reading his profile over and over.

Finally, without hesitation, she saw herself texting a confident, "Hi, how are you?" to the total stranger. Orianthi is a hopeless romantic who believes in unconditional love and happily ever after. She feels that everyone has a soulmate, and if one finds this soulmate in life, their love will eventually last forever. She was 32 years old, a short, curvaceous, stunning, and confident woman. She is vivacious, jovial, romantic, and intelligent. She appears intimidating, bright, but is quite bubbly, with a broad smile that cheers the most depressed of spirits. She is very provocative, passionate, fierce yet humble. She was an enigma. She is a mom to a 12-year-old girl from a previous short-lived relationship. She was recruited to work and emigrated to the United States 8 years ago from St Lucia with her daughter. She loved Florida because of its lack of extreme weather changes like other states. She was able to locate a few Caribbean stores for her favorite foods. It was a mere 3 hours' flight away from exotic St Lucia.

She loved being in South Florida though she gets homesick at times, especially around the holidays. She enjoys cooking, listening to music, a romantic walk along the beach watching the sunset, dancing, attending small gatherings, an occasional road trip, traveling, or relaxing at home and cruising. She is a critical care midwife who worked full-time as a charge nurse on a Cardiac Intensive Care Unit at the community hospital and works part-time as an adjunct nursing instructor. She currently holds a Bachelor's and Master's degrees in Nursing, specializing in the Nursing Education track. She was a single parent for 8 years before she met and married her ex-husband. Their marriage lasted for four years but could not survive the strain of her work such long hours, and her decisions to return to school. So when she was blindsided by her spouse's request for divorce, she decided to free him from his sagging ties to her.

Although she did not initiate the factors that led to her divorce, she contributed to it by working those extra shifts, getting busy with school. She did nothing to prevent the ultimate end of their union. She was sadly relieved that it was over. Now, they are civil to each other, and he is much happier with his other choice. She always wondered if she ever loved him? She is done with school, lonely, and is now ready to talk to another adult. This time around, Orianthi wanted to wait to meet her soulmate if he is still somewhere out there. It's been two years since her divorce, why has her soulmate not found her? She believes that maybe her soulmate got lost on his way to her and needed her to come in and rescue him. She always yearns for this happily ever after fairytale with her soul provider that her historical romance novels described. She craves these undying love she reads. She laid in bed, thinking of the caramel stranger and wondering what he was doing at that precise moment. As she drifted off to sleep, she silently prayed that the tall, mysterious stranger was real, available, exciting, and searching for her too.

Chapter 1

FEELINGS AWAKENED

Orianthi was awakened to the sounds of the rain on her windows, the flashes of lightning blazing the dark night sky, followed by roaring thunders in the distance. She loves rain, rainy nights, thunderstorms; she knows that's her likes are weird, but she cannot explain it. Again she thinks – Orianthi hates not being in love or not having this special someone to share her innermost thoughts with on such a stormy night. Orianthi misses the intimate tendencies that a night like this conjures. As Orianthi laid in bed savoring the rain, she was interrupted by a strange buzzing sound that she could not recognize at the time. For a millisecond, she wondered why her alarm buzzed on a Saturday morning? She looked around and identified the source of the weird sound. She reached for her phone and saw several notifications from the interracial dating site.

Imagined her surprised when she realized that there were three messages from her delightful, caramel, sexy stranger! Rain and thunder forgotten, she flipped over onto her back to eagerly access the messages. He responded to her, "Hi" with- "Hello." Her 'how are you?

With - "I am much happier now reading your messages." He then continued to announce that "He was happy she wrote to him, that he was new to the site." He thanked her for the ice breaker then informed her that, though he highlighted her profile as his favorite, he was too shy to write her and was hoping that she did. He introduced himself as NXavier Dimitri. 'NXavier,' the name rolled off her tongue seductively. She said his name out loud and wondered what his name would sound like in the throes of ecstasy? She had to literally pull herself away from this thought begrudgingly to reality, because it was much too soon for a lady like herself to think of 'ecstasy' with a random, though an enticing stranger, however, she could not help herself.

As the day went on, they both continued their questions and answers session of their "getting to know phase" of their interactions. She found herself preoccupied with her phone all day. What a difference a day makes!! She was happy reading about him and writing to him. For the next few days, she looked forward to every message from him. She learned that he was French, ' enchanteé! A French man, it meant he could whisper sweet nothings to her in French "trés sexy!" Orianthi chuckled. Orianthi was getting ahead of herself; she was already assuming that NXavier may know the French songs on her playlist that she had been longing to dance to with a French man. This also meant just maybe he was able to dance zouk. She could hardly wait to assess his playlist.

NXavier told her about his reasons for relocating to South Florida from Quebec with his family 6 years ago and how he was initially hired as a consultant Lockheed Martin but now currently works as an aeronautic simulation analyst for them. 'Quite impressive,' she thought. She knew nothing about his field but was excited to hear about his roles. He currently lives alone in Boca Raton. Orianthi was mentally calculating the distance from Weston to Boca Raton, which was 45 minutes away from her home. She questioned his reason for living alone and inquired about his family. NXavier texted that he was alone because he was recently divorced about 6 months ago, but shared custody of his two sons with his estranged spouse who returned to Quebec with his sons. He explained though he misses his boys, it was their mutual decision that their sons be raised in Quebec. Orianthi asked about how often he sees his son, he replied, "Every few months." He omitted to share with her the full extent of his relationship status. He mentally told himself that he would divulge those details if the need arises.

NXavier discussed his love for the year-round temperature of South Florida, how he enjoyed living so close to the beach, how peaceful the night sky felt compared to the busy city of Quebec's. He also loved the community, how comfortable he felt, and how quickly he adapted to living in Boca Raton. Orianthi was quickly becoming enchanted* with him and was quite fascinated with how relaxed and flawless their conversations flowed. He seems intrigued by her as she was with him. As the hours turned to days, he questioned her about her decision to leave a beloved Caribbean island for the United States. Though he had never been to St Lucia, he had been on a Caribbean cruise since he moved to Florida and loved exploring the islands immensely. He inquired about her passion for teaching, her love for cardiac nursing, her fascination with academia, and her family life.

She was amazed at their many commonalities. NXavier spoke French, English, and Spanish, she spoke English, Creole, and French. Like her, he loved rain and thunderstorms, dancing to Zouk, reading, cooking, and cruising. They shared similar tastes in music, movies, television shows, dreams, goals, they were both compassionate souls, but the tiebreaker was that they excited each other tremendously. He informed her that his ex-wife was a black woman, and he had always fancied himself with black women. Orianthi felt much better about them after his confession because she would hate to be just a 'passing' fancy to some stranger that she was wildly getting much too attached too after a mere few weeks. NXavier was looking forward to getting to know her and to see her beguiling smile in person.

When they finally exchanged telephone numbers, she was fascinated with his deep, waspy voice. He thought that the sound of her voice was soothing and priceless. They spoke for hours each night, and he was a breath of fresh air, eloquent, methodical, and engaging, like her; he was also a social injustice activist. They shared similar worldviews about the current political climate, immigration, access to healthcare and climate change, and advancements in research. They could communicate on any given topic and never get bored with each other. He was respectful, charming, well-read, and worldly. His voice was mesmerizing, he was a great communicator, a gentleman, he was perfect for her!

What more could a girl ask for? Although their schedules were quite hectic, she was extremely excited when he suggested that they meet. She blushed at the thought of meeting him and wondered what it would feel like to meet in person. They consulted their calendars and decided to meet in 2 weeks as he had a business trip planned to Seattle that weekend and wished to visit his sons in Quebec before he returned to South Florida. She felt a tinged of jealousy knowing to well that while he was away in the next 2 weeks, she may not experience such liberal access as she did when he was in Florida.

They continued their conversations throughout the week fervently, to compensate for his trip to Quebec and felt quite deflated after his last night in Seattle. She wished that she was going with him to Seattle. She fell in love with Seattle when she saw the movie *'Sleepless in Seattle'* and again while watching *'Frasier.'* She always loved seeing the constant rain through bay windows overlooking the Space Needle on *'Frasier.'* The picturesque scenery combined with the rain, and the fireplace always seems so cozy. The sensation felt from watching this show was the sole reason why she purchased a fireplace for her home in a high 80-degree temperature in Florida. Orianthi asked NXavier to describe his scenery from his window, yes it was raining as she daydreamed, and he too was able to see the tip of the historical monument from his suite. She was jealous!

He left Seattle on Monday after his conference and set out for Quebec and his family. He was excited to see his sons but felt a bit uncomfortable being home with Jocelyne, his wife, after speaking to Orianthi for the past months. What a contrast between 2 beautiful black women. NXavier wishes he was heading back to Florida instead, to their first date with Orianthi, but he really missed his boys. The first day dragged on for eternity for Orianthi. She had gotten so used to his constant text and impromptu short calls throughout the day and long calls at nights, that his absence was felt immensely. She longed to hear him, but she promised to keep her distance while he visited with the boys. It would be incredibly selfish of Orianthi to intercept on his own time with his sons, and she told him as much. She misses him tonight, she would have preferred to be on the phone having the deepest, mind-boggling conversations with him, instead of rereading their past discussions.

She drifted off to sleep to Princess Lover's singing" Dans *Ma Vie*" in a French concert on YouTube. She was dreaming; she was in bed cuddling with him, his arms laying over her full breast, with his muscular thigh over her. She could feel his hot breath on her neck, his voice whispering sweet nothings in her ear. She laid content in his arms, listening to music.

Suddenly, she became aware of his engorged member probing her. He pressed her hip into him to ensure that she felt his power. She heard him mumble some incoherent French words as he lightly massaged her globes. She felt wetter as his body pressed into her. He continued to thrust into her, his skin on her skin. She felt wetter with anticipation of him feeling her up. He massaged her nipples slowly as they responded to him shamelessly.

NXavier moved his hand to her thigh and grazed them with his fingertips, which sent chills up her spine. He then opened her moist chamber and lightly grazed her finger into her softness. Her body shivered from his touch. She enjoys him touching her in this private area, she closed her eyes aching and yearning to be fused by her delectable French Prince. His index finger settled on her knob, and middle finger pressed into her moist crevice. He withdrew his fingers as he fumbles with his engorged member. She shivered with anticipation, his skin felt so smooth on her naked skin, his kisses on her thigh sent heated electrical beams of heat down her spine. She laid in his arm shivering as she awaited his invasion, Orianthi felt his knob rest on her wetness and felt him open her soft lips, just as he entered her delicate moistened treasure she was jolted awake by the sound of an annoying ringing sound from her telephone.

Darn, she was only dreaming," she thought angrily, and who in God's heaven had the nerve to wake her from her sweet dream?? It was him on the phone; obviously, he was forgiven after hearing his deep voice. Orianthi felt a bit self-consciousness about her broken dream. She was grateful that he was too far away from her to see her bothered state. She felt so hot and disturbed, disappointed that he interrupted her dream but happy to hear his voice. She did not expect to hear from him until Saturday. He announced that he had arrived safely, and was about to set out of the airport. NXavier announced that his flight was uneventful, how he missed her already but was looking forward to seeing her the coming weekend. She remained relatively quiet as possible for fear he would notice her accelerated breathing. She almost wished that her dream was real, and he was here with her. As they hung up, she realized that she never told him about her sensual dream.

Chapter **2**

DISTANT EXPLORATION

NXavier sat in his service car on the ride home from the airport, staring out at the beautiful night skies. He surprised his family this visit; he loves the joys that fantastic holidays bring to the boys. He had not seen them since his appointment two months ago and was happy he got the time to be here. He missed the boys much more than he misses his wife, Jocelyne, of 20 years. He recalled the days when he used to be excited to go home to her, life was amazing then. He misses this Jocelyne, the soft, quiet, attentive girl who was forced to adopt a military- spouse lifestyle without him. He misses Jocelyne, who looked forward to his visits before the boys were born. He knows that being in the navy for so long, for their entire marriage may have created this unbreakable distance between them.

He loved Jocelyne, she is an amazing mom, she was a good wife to him then, he just wished their lives went further than being great parents. NXavier and Jocelyne were high school sweethearts who got married right before he set off to the navy at 19 years old. For the past 21 years of their marriage, they have been apart more than they have been together. The distance between them may have impacted their marriage immensely; they tried counseling when he eventually ended his service to the military, but they stayed together for the love of their boys Jade and Stephane.

The intimacy was missing, yes, but they respected each other. They were childhood friends, so they are quite loyal to each other; however, the love that existed in most relationships was lacking in their union. On his many visits home, he would initiate a form of intimacy, but her lackluster efforts made his interest dwindle off over the years. Now he refrains from attempting to avoid the constant rejections and was content with the situation of co-parenting. It's comfortable, it's routine, it was enough until now.

Jocelyne usually keeps herself busy with various social activities, spa treatments, book clubs, and weekend getaways with her friends, whenever he visits Quebec or even when he came home from his tours. So most of his visits would be spent with his kids uninterrupted. He never complained because he viewed her time away from the boys as her vacation for holding up the fort while he was on duty. He would sometimes plan family vacations, which would conflict with Jocelyne's plans, so now he only plans outings with his sons. The boys would continuously ask if mummy would come along on their family trips, and he would always explain that their mom had previously scheduled engagements. On many occasions, he has hinted on her visiting Florida on school breaks to reconnect with him; however, she usually had an excuse not to, so he finally stopped asking. He hates being away from them but staying home full time was driving him insane. He needed to work, he loved doing his job, and the tension at home, between Jocelyne and him, was beginning to affect the boys.

NXavier enjoys spending time getting to know his sons. He was away on tours for most of their significant milestones, so he would make up for the lost time by rolling around on the floor with them, taking them to the park, museums, zoo, water, cycling, and amusement parks. He enjoys tucking in his sons to bed and reading to them every night. On many occasions, he would sleep with the boys in their room. They love it when he is home. He was never away from them before unless he was deployed, until now. Once he was activated nationally within Quebec, his family traveled with him everywhere. They all moved to Florida when he started the new job; however, they were not thriving academically in the education system in South Florida as well as they did in Quebec given the language barrier, and as a result, the decision was made to have them move back to Quebec with their mother. He wishes that he could be with them daily, but his job keeps him away. Thanks to the advancement in technology, he can speak and see their cute faces daily and listen to specific activities of their days.

There was no love lost between Jocelyne and himself, no intimacy, no connection only the promises made by teenagers' decades ago. They had outgrown each other over the years and went out of their ways to avoid each other. They had never swayed away from the promise made to each other, but on those lonely nights away from home, he would crave a conversation. Their conversations lately mainly included discussion about the boys, and then phones are quickly handed over to the boys as she conveniently disappears into the next room. He wished that they could return to their previous life before the kids were born before they were married. They were both teenagers then, at least then they were in love with each other and worked well together. Now they work quite effortlessly at pretending to love each other in the company of others. They are civil with each other and would share air kisses on the cheeks on greetings and occasional hugs whenever the boys are in sight.

Since he began communicating with Orianthi, NXavier craves the feelings of a woman, inhaling her perfumed scent, feeling the softness of her body below him, his lips on hers, and being in a healthy loving relationship. He would be willing to improve what he has with Jocelyne, but he knows that it was not possible. He has tried futilely for many years. After his last trip home, he felt lonely and needed to fill this void with adult conversation. When he signed up on the dating site, he intended to connect with an adult, but not intimately, as he was not interested in a relationship. As a result, his attachment to Orianthi scares him a bit. He told himself he only needed someone to talk too. He was still conflicted about his plans for next weekend with Orianthi because he was dreadfully worried that upon meeting her, he may not be able to stay away from her.

Orianthi was a breath of fresh air, and though all their conversations remained platonic, he knew he needed to see her, to hug her, and craved to kiss her plump lips. He was drawn to her like a weak moth to a dangling flame. For the past two months, she was exhilarating, and it had become quite a struggle to keep himself away from her. He enjoys speaking to Orianthi, she is opinionated, passionate, and exceptionally well- versed. He was steadily drawn into a heated debate with her on every topic. She excites him; she had a fire that was unparalleled to anyone. He was mesmerized by her smile, and she was not afraid of a fight with him. She challenges him in ways no one in his profession, and personal life has ever done. He took this impromptu trip to confirm to himself that his relationship with Jocelyne was over. He will attempt to explore its future this week hence the surprise to catch her at home with no plans on a school week. He dreaded the upcoming 'tete a tete' with her and would ensure that the discussions would be held when the boys are out of the home.

The service car pulled into his driveway, and he pulled away from his thought to prepare for his boys. He opened the door amid huge squeals of joy from the boys. He completely forgot his dilemma and concentrated on his sons hugging on to each leg. Jocelyn stood at the door with a surprised look on her face *'why didn't he inform her that he would visit,'* she thought. He needed answers to this visit; the answers lay with Jocelyne. He hugged his wife and enquire about her wellbeing. She answered but volunteered no additional information. This was normal for them; he did not expect much in the way of reassurance since he FaceTime with his family twice daily. He was happy that She was preparing dinner, which meant he was not too late. Jocelyn is a fantastic cook. He went in for a shower, and the boys followed him inside. He redirected them to their gifts in his suitcase and could follow their squeals all the way to the hallway, where he abandoned his luggage.

His mind drifted to Orianthi, he missed her and wondered if she was thinking of him too. He sent Orianthi a short message before switching off his phone and realized how much he misses her cheerful voice on the other end of the phone. He knew that she would be in class at this time. NXavier hurriedly took his shower and joined his family for dinner. They dined on roasted garlic chicken, baked potatoes, Caesar salad, and fried rice.

As usual, the boys chatted throughout their meals, which allowed the adults very little time for one on one conversation. After dinner, his wife cleaned up while he gave the boys their bath and readied them for bed. It felt great hearing their bickering in person than on FaceTime. They were quite witty and loud, and he loves their constant debates, those kept him quite amused during their nightly rituals.

After they were both asleep, he went out in search of Jocelyne for a nightcap. He found her in their bedroom lying on a chaise lounge engrossed in a local reality show. NXavier asked if she would join him in a drink, and she nodded her head in agreement.

He poured Jocelyne a glass of her favorite Pinôt Noir and poured himself a cognac. He pulled a chair close to the lounge chaise and sat facing her to scrutinize her face for what he was about to do and say. She seems uncomfortable sitting so close to him. On a typical night, Jocelyne would watch television before bed, while NXavier would be on his laptop or reading in bed. Usually, they would be engaged in their own rituals until bedtime, then they would both be fell asleep on their respective sides of the bed, with no cuddling, no touching. He needed to change this routine this week.

He held Jocelyne's hand, brought it up to his lips, and kissed it whilst staring keenly at her face. She was tense at first but relaxed and smiled with an enquiring look on her face as to what his agenda was; she wanted to get back to her reality show; however, Jocelyne sensed he needed to talk to her. She was apprehensive of any conversation that would explore their status quo. Orianthi loves her life, the boys are well adjusted, they are healthy, excelling in school, and happy. She dreaded a conversation because she has never thought of changing a thing about their current status quo. It was perfect. She was raising her children; he provides for their needs. She loved her husband but was not in love with him. He never forces her to engage in any intimacy, she has her friends, her club, she is happy.

Jocelyne sat near NXavier and felt him kissing her arm, kissing her neck, attempting to kiss her lips, and she felt nothing. Until now, she had not thought of him being with her so intimately. They had not explored a physical relationship in over six months. Jocelyne does not consider herself frigid, but after twenty years, she believed that they had fallen into a comfortable pattern where sex between them was no longer explored or expected. She wondered what had come over him? Why the sudden interest in touching her tonight? She stared at NXavier and thought of their relationship, yes, he is a great father, a wonderful man, a fantastic provider, and he treats her like a queen. Maybe she too may have needed to explore their relationship. Perhaps he deserves some attention.

Jocelyne snapped out of her thoughts and searched NXavier's face. NXavier had joined her on the lounge chaise and was kissing her neck and cheeks but realized she was lost in thought and paused his advances to assess her interest. She did not encourage him to continue. Several questions swirled around in Jocelyne's head. *Why the sudden interest?*

What did he want? Why was he kissing her? Why the surprise visit? Is he okay?' None of those she asked out loud. She was lost in thought and did not realize that he had stopped kissing her neck and stood watching the flow of emotions on her face. *'Did he disgust her this much?'* He thought. NXavier stood up to refresh their drinks and came back to her chair then asked Jocelyne point-blank, *"Are you in love with me?"* She looked up at him, blankly in shock. *"Is kissing me so disgusting?"* He continued.

Jocelyne sat there in silence. She had never thought of a response to this question before. She needed to process the answers to those questions. She was still thinking of her reaction when she heard the door closed and realized NXavier was gone. NXavier felt that she needed the appropriate time to think about their life as much as he had over the past 2 months. So he needed to leave her alone to allow her to reflect on her thoughts. He walked over to an empty room, praying that he was not followed because he was no longer in the mood for a discussion tonight. He undressed down to his boxers and laid in bed, he then realized it was raining and reach for his phone. Orianthi did respond to his message and bid him goodnight. He stared at a smiling picture of Orianthi and felt a more profound need for her tonight than ever before. Being rejected by Jocelyne tonight was less painful because he now has someone who equals his interest in her. He kissed her smiling face on his screen as he fumbled at his hardness.

Oh, how he wished she was here lying next to him. He needs to feel her lying beneath him. Tonight he needed to release this pent up pressure building up inside him from the time he met Orianthi. He wished that he was dancing with her; Orianthi pictured himself undressing her curvaceous body; he imagined himself kissing her all over and hearing her sweet voice, encouraging him to kiss her gentle, velvety folds. Hmmmmmm, his tongue darted out to lick his dry lips. He stroked himself harder and tighter. He found himself enjoying the thoughts of pleasing her and felt his pressure built up at the idea of leaking her soft folds. The more he thought of her, the greater his influence felt. He thought he heard her ask him, *"eat me,"* as he erupted his juices into some nearby napkins. He laid spent, smiling at this image of him with Orianthi in this daydream. He took a quick shower, the sneaked into his sons' room to sleep. He drifted to sleep happy, content, and more relaxed than he had ever felt in years.

Chapter 3

UNEXPECTED DECISION

NXavier was awakened by the squeals of the boys as they realized their dad was asleep in their room. The boys took one look at the rain and were begging to stay home with him. It was a really dark, wet, gloomy day out, he wondered if it was raining in Florida, and how much Orianthi would have enjoyed this present weather. She would have loved it!

He missed having a conversation with her on their commute to work this morning. It was 7:00 a.m., so she was already at work, he thought. He will try to reach out to her later in the day. It was a school morning for his boys, though it was overcast outside he needed to discuss with Jocelyne whether to send the boys to school today. He was amazed at the boys' energy so early in the morning. He hugged the boys, ordered them to get ready for school, and smiled at their sad expressions as they left in search of breakfast.

He wished he could keep them at home on such a horrible day, too, but he needed some time alone with their mom. He required the boys at school because he wanted to continue his discussions from the previous night. He did not know how heated their argument would be and did not want to expose his sons to their parents fighting. They had never done so before, and he would be damned if they would start now. He walked into the room and realized Jocelyne was in the shower; however, the door was locked. She only locked the bathroom door if she did not want to be disturbed by him or the boys. NXavier enquired about the possibility of keeping the children at home through the closed door, and she confirmed that they would be attending school because it was a testing day. He showered, got dressed, and returned to the boys' room, and assisted them with getting ready for school.

The drive to school was longer than expected because of the weather. NXavier decided to quiz the boys on the material for their exam. After exams, he promised to withdraw them a bit earlier than scheduled to catch a movie with them, and their energetic spirit returned at that thought. On the drive home, his mind again wandered to Orianthi. He intended to continue his talk with Jocelyne, but he wishes in this rain he was driving home instead to be with Orianthi. Damn! He wished she was seated next to him, his hands cradling hers. He wondered why all thoughts of her always left him engorged. He pictured her waiting at a hotel for him, soft, ready, and wet. His need for Orianthi was so compelling that he imagined himself entering the room, walking towards her on the bed. He imagined pulling her to the edge of the bed on all fours and entering her roughly. His thoughts of this scenario made him throb painfully. He imagined her moaning with each deep thrust as he pulled over in his driveway. The rain was more torrential now, which trapped him in the car.

NXavier reclined the car seat and grabbed some napkins to free his painful throbbing shaft from its prison. The rain gave him the perfect avenue to sit back and allow himself the pleasure of enjoying Orianthi's sweet tight box. NXavier closed his eyes and imagined him long fingers grabbing Orianthi hips, pulling her to him as he roughly thrust into her. He imagined her moaning beneath him but begging him for more. He felt like he was deeper inside of her softness, her movements match his intensity, her juices coating his shaft. She was calling his name, he missed feeling this way, he missed being needed this way. He missed being in love and missed the throes of ecstasy he envisioned with Orianthi. He felt the pressure in his heard, his shaft throbbing and heard himself call out her name as they both collapse breathlessly in the bed.

He opened his eyes to the heavy raindrops on his windshield and was quite grateful for the privacy they provided him. He cleaned up, smiled, and left Orianthi a lengthy voice note on WhatsApp. He told her about the weather, his activities with his son and how much he wished she was right next to him, and wish he could give her a leisurely tour of his town. He omitted to tell her that his last impression of her was an image of her round butt, or how happy he felt a minute ago thrusting into her tight, wet folds. The heavy showers subsided for a second to allow him a chance to make a run for it. He runs into the house, soaking wet, and headed straight for a shower. He definitely needed a bath; he felt guilty, asking Jocelyne about her feelings for him while he can smell on himself the juices of his experience in the car with Orianthi.

NXavier left the shower feeling energized, refreshed, and virile. He found Jocelyn seated at the kitchen table reading a book. His breakfast was waiting on the table across from her. He sat down and started on his scrumptious breakfast while Jocelyne avoided eye contact with him. He asked her about the boys' schedules, issues at home that he needs to rectify before he leaves, but Jocelyne only answered the questions with monosyllables.

She dreaded the discussion that she anticipates will follow because she still had no clear answer for him. NXavier sensed her tension and thought it was better to discuss them now than prolong the inevitable. He repeated the same questions to Jocelyne and was not entirely surprised when she said no to both. She explained hesitantly how she loves him as a friend, as the boys' father, as a partner, but she was not in love with him in the biblical sense. Jocelyne also explained that she was not disgusted by his touch and apologized, but she was content with the status quo and was not interested in exploring those affections anymore with anyone. Orianthi just wanted to be left alone to raise her sons.

She stilled herself waiting for an angry retort and, she was surprised that he remained quiet. NXavier sat there in silence, replaying the answers from Jocelyne, was he in disbelief at her genuine responses? No! Unfortunately, he felt the same way about her but refrained from telling her as much. He was elated, to say the least, and was now happy to pursue his need for Orianthi. He felt lighter than he thought in years. He wondered if he could love someone the way he loved Jocelyn. As he thought of loving someone, Orianthi's face appeared in view, and he believes he might already be in love with her. He wished he was sitting across the table from Orianthi and not Jocelyne, feeding her the grapes from his plate and laying her on the table as he feasts on her juices. He stood up and walked to the enormous bay windows overlooking the city and stared at the raindrops on the nearby trees.

Jocelyne watched him at the window and wondered why he suddenly needed those answers from her, and why did he take her responses so calmly? *Will he ask for a divorce??* She asked. She could not continue to hide the truth from him. He deserved her honesty, if not for her, for the sake of their sons. She was petrified of this thought of him divorcing her, what would she do without him being around. She sometimes wished she loved him the way he deserves to be loved, but it was just not there anymore. He thought of going for a jog in the rain to cleanse him and removed the guilt he felt for wishing he was here with Orianthi. He needed to feel free to love her, he craved a balance between his current life and a new one with Orianthi, and somehow he thinks that the rain would hide his thoughts or erase it altogether. He decided to go for a run, got ready, and headed out. He had quite a lot to process at that moment, and he could not do so at home.

He loves the feel of the rain on his face and the clarity that the raindrops offered.

He would not ask Jocelyne for a divorce because he was worried about its impact on his sons. He lives in Florida, so it is easy to maintain the status quo without anyone getting hurt, Jocelyne, and Orianthi. At least now, he did not have to fuss and endure a tepid relationship with Jocelyne. He will continue to visit the boys and call them, but he will allow his interest in Orianthi to blossom. There was no clear path to Orianthi that did not include Jocelyne and the boys. As much as he wanted to be with Orianthi, he will refrain from divulging his current status to her at this time. Though he missed the stable relationship he had with Jocelyne, at 38 years old, he needed more. He stopped to give Orianthi a called and hoped she was free, but his call went to her voicemail. He smiled at the sound of her sweet voice on her message and realized that he really missed Orianthi. He left her a text message confirming their plans for Saturday evening.

He was finally free to feel excited, free to want her, open to love her in his own way without remorse, he was happy. He needed to feel loved, to be in love with someone, no matter the circumstances. He wanted to come home to someone, and make love to her and she to him. NXavier was haunted by dreams and images of Orianthi, how he wished she was here in the rain with him! He thought of the daydreams he had of her the previous night and the one in the car earlier and felt instant steering for her again. He wondered if she would allow him to kiss her on the first date. NXavier made a mental note to take her to an intimate club, which offers both a quiet dinner and dancing. He needed to feel her body pressed into him, arms around her, his cheeks close to hers. He needed to feel her on his skin. As he turned to run back to his home, he knew one thing for sure this was no longer his home.

Chapter 4

MISSING HIM

It was the fourth day of NXavier's trip to Quebec, and Orianthi was going through intense withdrawal symptoms. She missed him tremendously! Orianthi missed the sound of his voice, his concerns on her late commutes home, and his many texts to verify she was home. In the past few months, she had gotten quite inured to his daily texts, scheduled calls, short messages with in-depth conversations. His voice seems to calm her spirit, his mind in sync with hers. He had the knack to be powerful and soft in the same breath. He was forceful yet tolerant of her wimps, but his commands were not to be disobeyed. She loved his power over her. He was always stable in instances when she was weak, and he was her voice of reason when she had none. He possessed all the qualities she craved in a potential guy, he was caring, attentive, patient, supportive, and resourceful. It was impossible to be so attached to someone so soon, but she was!

He was charismatic, soft-spoken, slow to anger, he knew how to make her laugh and was very fascinated with her upbringing in St Lucia. Orianthi felt quite lonely tonight without NXavier. Since he was gone, she found herself continually staring at her phone for a text message from him and tripping over furniture to avoid missing his calls. So far, she had missed every one of his calls, though not intentionally. Orianthi is grateful that she did miss NXavier's calls because she can now play his voice notes and messages over and over again on the nights when misses him like she does tonight. When Orianthi suggested no calls while he was in Quebec with the boys and he did not discourage the idea, she was jealous, jealous of the fact that he had another life that he was not willing to share with her. She knows that the boys are living with their mom, so if NXavier did not encourage calls to him, Orianthi feels that it would be rude of her to initiate them. The last thing Orianthi wanted to do was to call NXavier in Quebec and create friction between him and his ex-wife just because she misses him. He will be back soon enough, she thought.

The past four days went by in a complete blur for Orianthi and, the days felt like an eternity. She wondered if NXavier misses her as much as she misses him. So far, she has received a few voice notes from NXavier, and a few missed calls none at nights though, which to her, happens to be the worst part of his absence. If he were in Florida, they would be on the phone talking until the wee hours of the morning or both too exhausted to remain awake. NXavier did leave a message on Tuesday, confirming their date for this Saturday and said that he is due in South Florida on the late flight on Friday. He chose this new flight because he wanted to spend as much time as possible with his sons. She wondered about his life in Quebec, he talks about the boys quite often but seldom discussed his ex-wife, which she was not interested in hearing about anyway. Orianthi wondered if he will ever open up about this aspect of his life. She thought to herself that she has her past as well, so she knows that prying may be unwelcomed in some instances. Yes! Orianthi would like to know everything about him but thought not having met NXavier, she should respect his privacy if he decides not to divulge his secrets, and he will do so when he is ready.

Outside seems very dark, which mirrors her mood tonight. The sky was overcast, a few claps of thunder heard but no rain. The leaves on the trees were; still, no breeze came in from her open window. She prayed for rain because she knows that NXavier loves the rain as much as Orianthi does, and if Orianthi couldn't have him tonight, at least she could have the rain, something near and dear to their hearts. She stared at the few stars left in the sky and wished that NXavier was watching the same stars wherever he was. A flash of lightning brightly illuminated the night sky, and she continued to stare at the same spot, patiently waiting for more lightening. She wandered out onto her porch, and the warm air that greeted her was soothing but still too humid for a summer night. Suddenly she felt the first few raindrops on her face and lifted her face to explore more as if the rain knew of her need and came to rid her of her loneliness. She was elated! She loves to fall asleep to the sounds of rain on her windows. Maybe tonight, she will finally sleep without continually waking up to check her phone for possible messages from NXavier.

She became quickly bored and very distracted since he was gone. Although she has tried various means of diversion, all failed in comparison to her first sultry dream of him. NXavier seems to be the only one who can reach her through her lunacy. Her mind persistently wanders in search of his face, and she is regularly daydreaming of being kissed all over by him. She wished he was here! Oh, how she wishes that she could extract him from her brain cells and hold on to him on her dark and when she misses him. She wished she could stay in the rain but decided against the idea because if the lightning. She aches to dance and be kissed in the rain by NXavier. She wished he was with her.

She walked back into her room and closed the door. She wiped the raindrops off her skin, then left the curtains ajar to see more of the lightning flashes in the sky, and headed to the shower. She was about to jump into the shower, but the glistening, bubbling waters of a Jacuzzi bath beckoned her. She was mentally running out of reasons to avoid laying in its beautiful blue relaxing bubbles. Why not, maybe the bubbles would relax her and give her new ideas to pass the time. She smiled at the thought of pleasuring herself in the tub tonight. She ensured all doors were secured, grabbed a towel, her favorite toy, shed her clothing, dimmed the lights, and wanders into the heated waters fully naked, and sank in. The soothing water was heavenly as it encircled her voluptuous body. She allowed the heated tub to cover her tired shoulders. She wished he was in here with her to rub her aching muscles. She closed her eyes and welcomed the soothing sounds of the pump. The bubbles vibrated around her body; she enjoyed the water tingling her arms, butt, legs, inner thighs, and nipples.

She opened her legs and encouraged the sprays on her clean-shaven crevice.

Her knob was responding to the assault of the spray, and her body started to crave for NXavier's long fingers. She imagined that he was sitting in the Jacuzzi with her straddling him. She pictured his engorged member at her innermost center. She found herself involuntarily squeezing her nipples. One hand moved to her hungry heated mold. She lightly touched her swollen epicenter. The other fingers circled her heated orifice. She pictured him sucking and licking her clit at the edge of the pool. She slipped her middle finger in and out of her hole, enjoying the exhilarating sensation that spread over her entire body. Damn, she misses this man! A sigh escaped her pursed lips. She bit on her bottom lip and brought the toy to her burning mound. She rubbed the tip on her swollen folds, ignoring the tenderness then slip it lower to her aching hole. She slowly opened her legs wider to facilitate its entry.

She slowly inched the hardened tool inside of her while rotating her hips in the water. She finally got its full length in and allow her body to adjust around it. She increased the pace of adapting to the toy. Orianthi imagines NXavier inserting the dildo into her and felt flushed all over at the thought. She relaxed, closed her eyes to enjoy her handiwork. It didn't take long for the combination of Orianthi's ideas of NXavier, the warm jets on her clitoris, and the tool inside of her to send her to the height of her needed release. She laid there spent wondering what their first kiss will be like. She got out of the tub and readied herself for bed. The thunderstorm continued on outside, she felt much better than she had felt all week. She was now excited and thinking about their date, praying that the chemistry matched the intensity of her need for him. She grabbed her discarded laptop and attempted to grade her student's assignments to no avail. Even after an orgasm, she still craved for him.

She reached for her phone and stared at NXavier's profile picture and combed through their messages. She would give anything to be with him tonight, in his arms, being kissed by him while they stare at the lightning and listening to the rain. She really wished they had kissed already, so the kisses she envisioned would not just be a figment of her sordid imagination. She hoped NXavier was in the same hemisphere or time zone to run into his arms, and he was unrestricted to run to her. Yes, she would have welcomed his seductive voice tonight, whispering sweet nothings to her over and over. She misses him, making her laugh about everything else but allowing her to vent about the miles of empty space between them. *Is he thinking of her tonight? Does he miss her? Does he think of her in those sensual terms?* Orianthi was left with a hundred unanswered questions about him. *Why is she so intrigued by him?* Her only answer is that she hankers the distraction his mental image envisages. He haunts her wakening thoughts and directs her passionate dreams. She could hardly wait to be with him on Saturday because her feelings for him are unrelenting!

She had a great night's rest and thought she would venture out to the store after work to grab some supplies since she would not be free on Saturday for her regular errands. She left her job early and decided to shop at the nearby supermarket. Since the store was not her regular grocery store, she spent an extended amount of time trying to locate the necessary items on her list. She went to the fruit and vegetable stand to get some pears and plums, her favorites. She was busy consulting her list and did not see the stranger next to her, they both reached for the same pear at the same time, and upon touching each other's hands, they felt this electrical current went through their hands. They dropped the fruit and withdrew their hands, and to their dismay, all the fruits cascaded down to the floor. In their embarrassment, they both bent to pick the fruits off the floor. She was in yellow scrubs and sneakers, hair pinned up in a ponytail, face looking freshly scrubbed with a light touch of Victoria Secret Satin Gloss adorning her full lips. He was in well fitted blue jeans, and Nautica yellow shirt complete with a pair of Clark's Loafers.

They absentmindedly pick up the pears in silence, embarrassed by the commotion it created. They were both tired, Orianthi she after a long 12-hour shift, and NXavier just getting off a long 5-hour flight from Quebec. They were impatiently trying to get home without this current incident. They hurriedly placed the fruits back on the stand and admire their handiwork. She turned in silence and walked away from him, leaving her keys at the fruit stand. He was about to leave when he sported her keys and was surprised to see a St Lucia key ring hanging from the bunch. NXavier picked up the keys and followed in the direction which she turned and found her two isles over at the wine section of the store, looking the bottle of pinot noir.

NXavier was about to speak to her when he realized how familiar she looks, he gazed at her speechlessly, speculating if it was actually his

Orianthi! He glanced down at the key ring in his hand and wondered if he was so lucky. He was not ready to meet her now, but she was so beautiful and confident, he felt intimidated by her. Why would Orianthi be at this store of all stores? Was it fate? Could this really be her? Orianthi placed the wine bottles into her cart and felt uneasy like she was being watched. At first, she thought it was another shopper who witnessed her fruit debacle earlier, so she ignored and continued to shop. She moved to the frozen food section but could not shake the feeling that she was really being watched, she took a beeline to the cash register to pay for her items. The cashier said something to her which made her smile, NXavier was at the next cashier over from her but could not stop himself from staring at her in astonishment! They had plans to meet the following night, and here she was shopping. NXavier thought that she was prettier in person, he wished that he could freshen up before he spoke to her, but there was no time since she was headed outside to the car.

Orianthi walked to her push-start car, expecting the door to open as usual, but the door did not. She never uses her key to open her door, so what was the issue tonight? She explored her bag in search of her keys and wondered why her car door would not open? She saw no keys and mentally tried to retrace her step, wondering when did she last saw her keys? Angrily, she turned around to walk back into the store and clumsily bumped into someone firm chest as the stranger wraps his arms around to steady her fall. She hastily apologized to the stranger, embarrassed at how clumsy she was tonight, and tried to detach herself from his firm grasp, yet his strong arms remained tightened around her waist. She inhaled the scent of his captivating Versace cologne and closed her eyes in exasperation in an attempt to pull herself away from this insolent stranger, but he held her firmly to his chest. She was about to knee him in the groan when she heard him say, "Hello, Orianthi."

Chapter 5

CHANCE ENCOUNTER

Orianthi froze, hearing her name from the stranger. She was startled by the sound of the impudent stranger's voice. Why are his hands still around her, and how does he know her name?

She quickly looked down at her chest to see if she was still wearing her name tag from work. No, she remembered taking it out in the car before she went into the store. She realized this was the same man at the fruit stand, she did not interact with him, but she recognized his attire then. She is fascinated by NXavier not blind, so yes, she saw an impeccably dressed man. *Did he follow her? Was he the one watching her at the store? Did he purposefully throw the fruits in there earlier? Why does this stranger's voice paralyze her? NXavier was on a flight back from Quebec, so why this stranger sounding like him?*

NXavier was still holding her, watching the fleeting expressions on her face as she tried to connect the dots. He loved the coconut-scented in her hair, he loved whatever fragrance she was wearing and how her voluptuous body felt in his arms. Most of all, he had in his arms for the first time around the culprit who had been creating these involuntary upheavals* in his life and mind of late.

He tightened his arm around her with his hands resting on the small of her back. Her pics did not lie. She was curvy. He could hardly wait to kiss her, NXavier thought as his eyes rest on her full seductive glossy lips. He could feel himself hardening. Yes, he was still holding her. Orianthi pulled out of her trance as she heard the car's door ding, signaling her key was near. She couldn't believe her first words to the hated stranger were, *"Do you have my keys?"* This man was still holding her, pressing her body into his firm chest, his strong arms felt like steel around her waist and his hands comfortably resting on hip, yet she was thinking of her keys. "Yes, yes!" he stammered. At that moment, his voice registered, and she looked up at his smiling face. *"NXavier,"* she whispered. *What was he doing here? He was with her from the fruit stand,* she thought. She had a million questions, but all evade her at the moment as she stared up at his face, anger replaced by a deep blush.

He told that she had left her keys at the fruit stand, and he followed her out when he realized it was her. Orianthi was still at a loss for words, and he noticed, so he continued talking. She was not hoping to meet him until tomorrow. She decided to shop tonight so she could be up late enough to speak with him as they usually do, but here he was, his arms wrapped around her waist. NXavier told her he got an earlier flight because the boys had a school dance to attend. He did not tell her that he could not be away from her any longer. NXavier further explained how he stopped at this store because he was starving and was not prepared to cook when he arrived at his home. He finally released his grip on Orianthi, and she was able to get her voice back. She took a step back to really get a good look at her stranger. He was taller than she expected, she wished to run her fingers through his thick hair, he was talking, but she was too mesmerized by his nearness to him to hear anything he was saying. She was no longer in his arms, but she could still feel her body resting on his. He was very tall, intimidating, charismatic, and looked terrific. When he looked at her face and licked his lips, which sent an electrical current through her entire body. She wondered what his kiss would feel like upon seeing the tip of his tongue.

NXavier smiled like he could read her mind, and she blushed for her indiscretion. He then stretched out his hand to formally introduce himself, and her soft hand disappeared in his long fingers. He needed to touch her again, so he thought by presenting himself, at least he could get to touch her hand. He offered to put her groceries in the trunk while she inquired about his trip. He moved around effortlessly for someone his height. He adjusted the rear door of the car to accommodate his height, then secured her belongings while they talked like old friends. It was easier to talk to him now that he was not leering at her and licking his kissable lips. He left her for a second to place his groceries in his truck. He returned to her and suggested they visit the Olive Garden in the plaza for dinner. She looked down at her attire, and he reminded her that they could order the foods and drive somewhere romantic to eat in the car. She agreed, as every second spent with him was a pleasure. She called to inform the sitter that she was running late, and had a short conversation with her daughter before joining him in his truck.

They collected their meals from Olive Garden, and he drove in search of a perfect spot. They took his truck and drove to a beautiful park about 10 miles from where they met. He occasionally stole glances at her and caught her doing the same as they both instantly looked away. He was grateful that they had chosen this exact store because their experience at the fruit stand gave them their perfect impromptu meeting tonight. He loved how comfortable she appeared to be around him, how down to earth she was, she was indeed beautiful, he thought. She had a feeling of 'déja vu,' it felt as if she had experienced this scenario before. He asked about her day, and why she chose this specific store? If she had not left her keys, he would have never realized, he was so close to her and would have not seen her. Before long, they were discussing their fiasco at the pear stand, and they were laughing hysterically like teenagers about it when he pulled into the park. He parked the truck with the trunk facing a gorgeous illuminated pond emanating from a majestic man-made waterfall. NXavier exited the car and placed their meals on the trunk of his vehicle then walked around to open her door for her. He opened the door but stood right in the doorway to help her out, which made getting by without pressing into him impossible.

He rested his face on hers, inhaling her intoxicating scent while she closed her eyes, thinking NXavier was about to kiss her, but he did not. He paused, took some deep breaths to compose himself to avoid things from getting out of control before it gets off the ground. His feelings for this woman who was one inch away from him was undeniable. When he looked at her, he melts; he was protected from her charm over the phone, but in person, he felt powerless around her. He wished that he could pull those short ample caramel thighs of hers and wrap them around his waist and take her right there. No! He calmed himself, he will not rush this! He does not want a fling with her, he wants her to be so in love with him that when he eventually reveals his current status with Jocelyne, she will have no choice but to agree to stay with him because she would not be able to live without him. He knows that he is dishonest with her, his guilt was killing him, but every time he looks at her, NXavier knows this is the only option left. He could not lose her on a technicality when every nerve ending of his was begging to kiss her, to be near her, to be inside of her. This will be much more difficult than NXavier envisions. He felt like a man who just broke out of jail after being incarcerated for a decade. He was consumed by her.

He inhaled deeply and pulled his face from hers without kissing her, and again, she felt slightly disappointed. NXavier placed his arms around her the help her down, she slid down his body to the ground, and he held her firmly to him for an eternity. When he released her, she almost felt lonely being away from the arms she was craving to hold her. She was flushed and stammering on her words like an idiot as he smiled and walked to the back of the truck. He climbed in and opened a blanket that he had picked from the Cleaners on the way to the store. He jumped out of the trunk, lifted her up, and placed her on the back of the trunk. She dished out their foods to avoid all eye contact and felt very happy, while he fixed their drinks, Orianthi's body was shamelessly hoping he put the glasses down and ravish her right here in the trunk. They both seem uneasy as they attempted to talk throughout their meals. They dined on some shrimp Alfredo with Cesar salad and a Chateau Ste. Michelle Riesling followed by the order of Tiramisu, which they shared while they silently stared at each other, wishing they were in a private park licking the Tiramisu or the wine off each other.

After dinner, they cleared up, and he placed his hands around her shoulder and pulled her closer to him as they snuggled together. They talked about their childhood. Orianthi told him about her trips to Martinique and her love for the French island; NXavier regaled her about his many visits to France to see his grandparents, about missing his parents who now reside in France to be close to his maternal grandmother who was currently ill. He told her about how his conservative parents did not approve of his ex-wife, so they have not been around much to see his sons. He seemed sad telling her about his family, so Orianthi reached out and squeezed his hand. She snuggled a little closer to comfort him and rested her head on his shoulder, inhaling his sweet musk. She knew already that he was an only child, and the thought of his parents not being around to love his boys because of his choice of the wife must be painful for him. She wondered how they would feel about her? She felt sad thinking they probably would not like her too because she was black. He did not tell her the reason why his parents did not approve of Jocelyne was that his mom was convinced from day one that Jocelyne did not love him, and he kept away to avoid confirming his mother's theory for the sake of his sons.

Speaking to him was easy, they had more similarities than they thought before. NXavier was intrigued by Orianthi's perseverance and all that she had accomplished though she had quite a humble beginning. He was saddened by some of her struggles but was quite grateful for her efforts, which led her to him right here, right now, and he was not the best choice for her at this time. She deserves to be cherished, loved, adored as someone's wife, but could not bear the thought of Orianthi with anyone else. He was amazed by how much he was enjoying her company. Orianthi loved the feel of his arms around her shoulders, she felt safe. They stared up at the night sky above, looking at the stars and wishing that the stars would make all their dreams come true. NXavier pulled her onto him as he laid beneath her, his hands resting leisurely on her hips. He needed her, he wanted to lay there all night with her, he never wants to be away from her again. Her body shivered at the thought of making love to him, and he asked if she was cold, and she nodded. He wrapped the blanket around them and stared at her face and her lips., and which she was straddling him. Again those her succulent lips beckoned, but he had no intention of kissing her tonight or any time soon. NXavier's goal is to get her to fall madly in love with him, and he would not jeopardies this by kissing her on their first encounter like he was not a gentleman.

She laid wrapped in his arms, sharing their innermost thoughts, now that she was here in his arms, he could hardly wait to see her again tomorrow. They discussed their plans for tomorrow, but he refused to divulge his plans for their second meeting regardless of how much she probed, he wanted to surprise her. She tried bribing him with a kiss if he would tell her. He smiled sheepishly* at the prospect of kissing her but refused anyway. Instead, NXavier told her that if he kissed her now, he was afraid that she would not show up for their date the next day, she laughed. Inwardly, he knew on no uncertain terms that if he tasted her full lips at this stage, there would be no turning back. She accepted his refusal; however, the thought of him kissing her, pleasing her, or undressing her crossed her mind. She became very conscious of her weight lying on him and asked whether she was too heavy, and he discouraged any thought of her moving off him. She did not fight the idea because she enjoyed being in those powerful arms; he just held her, knowing that at some point soon, he would need to release her and take her home. They remained at the park oblivious of the time. When the sky above appeared overcast, he informed her that she would need to get home before her beloved rain.

It was time to take her back to her car, NXavier helped her down from the truck but held firmly on to her. Orianthi wrapped her arms around his neck as she clung to him, suspended in mid-air. He looked at her searching her face for some sort of approval to ravish her. She was sensed his need and blushing under his scrutiny. NXavier loved that; at least she was less intimidating in his arms. He lifted her chin and stared at her lips, he craved to kiss her, but not tonight. When he does kisses her, he thought, he would need to savor this first kiss. He instantly stiffened at the thought of kissing her immediately and held on to her more firmly so she can feel his enlargement. She felt his swollen member and smiled, enjoying her effects on her enchanting companion. He finally allowed her to glide down his hardness but held on to her like he needed to cling to her for strength. He kissed her forehead and held her to him a little longer until a few drops of rain had them running to the car.

He drove her to her car but thought it was much too late for her to be home bringing in groceries from the car, so as they pulled up next to her car, NXavier informed Orianthi that he would be following her home to ensure that she got home safely. On the way home, Orianthi called to tell the sitter that she was close by and that she was free to leave. When she got back, she tried to get the groceries out of the car, but he heard nothing of it. Being the gentleman that he is, NXavier escorted her inside, then proceeded to carry all her groceries into the house. Orianthi went in to check on Lianii, her daughter, who was fast asleep, she kissed her goodnight, tucked her in, and went back out to say goodbye to NXavier. Orianthi offered him a drink, but he refused, saying he needed to get home as it was late. He took her hand as she walked him to the door, hugged her one more time and drove off, promising to call her later. Orianthi walked into the kitchen to put away her supplies. She smiled at the events of the day. When she was finished in the kitchen, she did a video call with her best friend Mia to regale her about the encounter with her stranger. She was engrossed in her conversation with Mia describing her prince charming surprised meeting when she heard the doorbell rang.

Orianthi kept Mia on the phone for security as she walked to the door, and to her bewilderment when she opened the door, NXavier was on her doorstep. Before she could utter a word, he pulled her to him roughly and captured her lips in the deepest kiss of her life. She was weakened by his lips on hers, he released her breathless body, and looked down at her face and kissed her again. He seemed angry, Orianthi thought, as she looked at him. He was crippled by her, he tried to drive to his home, but all he could think of was how tempting her lips looked. He was haunted by her lips already; all he knew was that he needed to taste them. Why couldn't he continue to drive home as he planned? Why couldn't he hold off until tomorrow to kiss her? She was supposed to fall for him, not the other way around, now he had blown off his only leverage on the first night, he thought angrily. He looked down at her puzzled face and pulled her to him again. NXavier was not prepared to tell her the effects she had over him, so he just pretended that he had forgotten to kiss her goodnight, so he came back to do so. Forgetting Mia on the phone, Orianthi smiled as she rested her head on his chest, listening to his beating heart. It was not long before his lips found hers again, hungrily.

Chapter 6

ENCHANTED ENDEAVORS

For the next few weeks, Orianthi and NXavier were inseparable unless he was away for work, visiting his boys, or she was busy with Lianii. He dotted on her, and she loved spending time with him. On the days they could not be together in person, they would be on the phone. He was her dream come true, and she was his second chance at love. On their second date, she met him at Sage French Cafe for brunch in Fort Lauderdale, occupying a cozy, corner, shaded patio table. NXavier and Orianthi were so enthralled with each other that they failed to see a change of guest from lunch to dinner and left at closing with arms wrapped around each other and a generous tip to their patient waitress. They occasionally paused to kiss each other senseless throughout their meals and were oblivious to others around them. Until today, they were never at a loss for words before, and when he took her home that night, he kissed her deeply at her door but did not ask to come in.

On the third date, NXavier took Orianthi for a helicopter ride over South Florida for a picnic. The basket was packed with assorted desserts, cheese, cold cuts, biscotti, and chilled, non-alcoholic champagne. She was in awe to realized he was the pilot, and they were all alone. NXavier was saving this surprise, so he never divulged that he was an experienced pilot as he wanted to see the shock on her face when she found out. The look of amazement was priceless! He thought as he greeted her with a kiss. Orianthi was nervous at first since she had never been on a helicopter before. He talked to her calmly, kissed her a few more times, and kept her talking to distract her. Once they were airborne and she was relaxed, he hinted that she helped with their picnic. She fed him while he flew the aircraft, with NXavier singing along to music from his playlist. He had a remarkable voice. Some songs were French songs that they both loved, so she enjoyed every second of it. Afterward, Orianthi decided to sit back to relish the fabulous scenery below as he became her excellent tour guide.

For the next few months, they fell into a comfortable routine, where they worked on weekdays and spend their weekends together, getting to know each other. They had not slept together, and Orianthi wondered why he hesitated. She wanted him so badly, and he always seemed to develop a bulge whenever they were together; however, he always seemed to contain himself and not cross that line. He was a perfect gentleman; he would kiss her, flirt with her, brush up against her and press her body into his but never seduced her or ravish her like she craved. It was apparent he was in no hurry; however, his actions were torturous. The previous weekend he took her to Bagatelle, a restaurant on South Beach, for an exquisite dinner and dancing. They danced sensually to their favorite Zouks for hours after dinner. He was an outstanding dancer. She wanted the night to last forever. Between the dancing and the kissing, he seems flushed and bothered. She was sure that he would have pulled her over on the side of the freeway and ravish her in the car, but he held it in.

One weekend, he surprised her with tickets to a Rihanna concert. After the show, they spent the rest of the night on the beach waiting to watch the sunrise. Laying on the sand, talking to him, and watching the sunrise with him made her realized how much she loved him. NXavier was so thoughtful and caring, he made loving her so effortless although he never said the words to her, she knew that he did. He had done so much for her that she decided to surprise him with movie tickets one weekend. She chose just the right theater for a sensual evening as their perfect surprise. They went to a private screening of a movie at the IPIC theatre in Boca Raton. They walked into their private room, ushered in by their personal valet. She paid for the entire room so they could be alone. He assisted her on a cozy recliner and sat next to her. The valet offered them a thick fleece blanket to snuggle under and a menu. She knew what she wanted already, so she barely glanced at the menu. The valet brought in their drinks and gave them a remote control to summon him for their meals and refresh their drinks.

Upon exiting the room, the valet turned off the light, which creates a perfect ambiance for what she had in mind. The minute he was gone, NXavier pulled her over his firm body to kiss her. The movie started in the background but did nothing to curb their need for each other. NXavier kissed her face, her neck, her bare shoulders with such hunger, as his hands run down her back, spine, hips, and thighs. She had on a beautiful, long, green floral sundress, but no panties, which made it easy to explore her curvy body in the dark. When he realized that she had no undergarment on, a soft guttural moan escaped his lips forcibly, and he kissed her roughly for torturing him. Orianthi could feel his need for her and pushed her hand between them to stroke his throbbing manhood. He brought his lips back to her, hungrily as she continued rubbing his clothed member. She longed to feel him buried to the hilt deep inside of her. NXavier was quivering beneath her from his deep need for her. He loved her unconditionally, but they had never discussed the possibility of her falling for him.

He had flowers delivered to her home and classroom at least once a week. He found out that she loves Hallmark greeting cards, so he flooded her mailbox weekly, with those from a secret admire. Orianthi knew that they were from him and cherished them lovingly. NXavier knew that on her busy days at work, she would skip meals to catch up, so he ensured that meals were delivered to her while she was at work. He had all angles of her life covered to satisfy himself that she needed nothing. Orianthi loved the way he showered her with his love. She was petrified to get too attached to this fairytale because she knew he was everything she ever wished for or dreamt of but never thought was possible. He was better than all the Knights in Shining Armors that she read about in all those romance novels. Now she had her ghost, her Prince Charming in the flesh, and she loved him.

She slid herself off him and unbuttoned his shirt to feel the hairs on his firm chest, as he took a sip from his drink. As her fingers grazed his nipples, he flinched from the electrified current soaring through his entire being. Orianthi excused herself and went to the washroom to freshen up. NXavier was not sure how much more of this he could endure. Every second spent with her was pure torture. Every time she touched NXavier's skin, he desired to devour her. His restraints were wearing off, his feelings for her were intoxicating, how did he let it get so bad? He longed to fill her up, he craved to lick her all over, NXavier ached to show her how much he loved her. He wondered how she felt about him? He was waiting for an indication from her that she loved him too before he buried himself in his love for her. He needed her to be in love with him in every sense of the word. On her way back in, she summoned the valet for some Bailey's on the rocks, then whispered that he put a "Do Not Disturb" sign on their door and left the valet with a huge tip to seal her demand.

She walked back to the recliner with her freshened drink, took a sip, and leaned over to kiss him. He loved the taste of the Bailey's on her tongue. He loved to suck her tongue. He wished he was tasting her sweet nectar right here. She removed his shirt and lay them on a nearby chair. She could see his bulge and could hardly wait to feel him in the darkened theater. She could not believe they were finally alone. Alone to hug, to kiss, to make love to each other. She could not wait for a second longer to be in his arms. She laid on him and began to kiss his neck. Orianthi felt like she was in a dream, floating above and looking down at them happily. It was everything she ever dreamt of. He was hard, her body felt soft and cradled in his arms. He kissed her forehead, and her insides turned into butterflies. She clung to him for support because she was weakened by his kisses. His soothing voice comforted her as he continued to kiss her neck, her cheeks, and back to her neck.

Orianthi laid on his chest, listening to his heartbeat. She was still quite nervous because unclothed, he was much hotter than anticipated. She envied his calmness and wanted to shake herself senseless for behaving like a naive virgin. He removed her dress patiently, although he wished to rip it off her body. He gazed at her nakedness like he was in a trance. NXavier felt so heated he forced himself to calm down and stared at her; otherwise, he would have erupted too soon. He touched her naked skin lovingly, and her body responded shamelessly. She could feel her juices drenching, overflowing from her folds, and spilling onto her thigh. When he finally kissed her lips, she prolonged their kisses and found herself continuously drawn to his succulent lips. He kissed her forehead, cheeks, and neck, and his kisses burned her skin.

Orianthi expected her body to hold off and exercise some form of self-control, but her traitorous body betrayed her into a powerful orgasm before NXavier could even penetrate her, leaving her breathless as she collapsed in his arms. He wanted to shoot his volcano to but will hold until he is buried in her softness. His scent filled her nostrils, she breathed profoundly calming the raging war between her legs. She reminded herself that they were in a public place and were probably being watched. This thought only fueled her to hastened her plans and take care of the starving NXavier. She licked her dry lips to moistened them and calm her nervousness. NXavier fingers rubbed her tight shoulders and her body, which was pulsating awaiting, hungrily for his deep invasion. He lifted her off his body and placed her to his left side, then lifted her thigh and put it over his legs.

NXavier rubbed her ample thighs until his fingers found her wetness. He long to lick those juices off her thick lips. He opened her delicately and located her knob and stroke it. She could feel his engorged poll pressing into her flesh. She reached behind her and squeeze the pulsating phallus; she felt his other hand, which was kneading her globes, released her breast as she felt him pull down the zip of his jeans, freeing his tortured beast. She felt his size and wondered if she would be able to accommodate his massive girth. His finger left her knob and open her lips until his long fingers located her epicenter and pushed a long slender finger inside her wet folds. He felt her withering under his touch, which drove him insane.

NXavier brought a finger to his lips and tasted her off his fingers. He had not felt such delicacies in years. She was just what he needed, who he wanted, and who he loves. He attempted to insert two fingers in but could not and realized as much as he needed to fill her up; he should be gentle with her. He guided his hardness to her velvet opening and gently penetrated her secret garden. She opened her leg a bit wider to wrap her leg around his thighs, allowing him to enter her slowly at first until her tightness adjusted to his width, then with one deep thrust, he buried himself inside her welcoming folds. When he finally filled her up, she wanted to resist for a second out of principle, but her body just needed him to continue those deep thrusts. He held her hips firmly and pounded into her tight crevice. She loves him in her, on her, below her, touching her, penetrating her. She understood at that moment how much her body ached for his touch. It was not long until another orgasm floored her drained body.

He continued his deep trust throughout her orgasm, which brought her to the highest heights. She spent an eternity with him filling her up with his hott, hard rod until he erupted deep inside of her wanton body. They remained in position until she handed him a towel to clean up. He withdrew from her slowing to avoid making a mess and rolled on his back. He was still erected and throbbing. NXavier was shocked as Orianthi bent over and brought his throbbing rod to her soft, warm lips. Her lips fitted around him, and she sucked him efficiently until his tart juices flooded her throat. She swallowed the load and lifted her head. NXavier pulled her to him and kissed her lovingly as he whispered, "I love you" to her. To his astonishment, Orianthi said she loved him too. At this precise moment, he knew that he would die if he could not be with her. They both smiled at the thought of being in love with each other. Orianthi wanted to stay in his arms forever if only she could, but not right here, the movie would be over soon.

They got dressed hurriedly and straightened up. Orianthi folded the discarded blanket and placed the soiled towel in her bag. NXavier left the valet an excellent tip as they sneaked out of the theater unseen. As NXavier laid in bed that night, she recalled their escapade earlier and blushed. He called to say goodnight and thank her for an unforgettable night. He fell asleep before hanging off the phone. She laid in bed, craving him more now than before. She dreamt of him in her bed, that night, him sleeping with her and woke up aching for him immensely. She loves him and thought that he was hers, and she was his, even more now. She misses him dearly and could hardly wait to welcome him inside her folds again where he belongs.

Chapter 7

RAINY DAY PLEASURES

Orianthi woke up to a wet and cloudy Sunday morning, Lianii was over by her Aunt Mia from the night before. She will come home later when the weather permits. Orianthi laid in bed, staring at the rain through her windows and wishing her Prince Charming was with her. Images of her public scene with him the night before came flashing back. She cannot believe how brave she was the night before. She hoped that no one saw them or recorded their escapade. Although it was much too late for second thoughts, it was their first night, she blew NXavier's mind; so no misgivings about her actions now. She reached for her phone to say hi to Mia and to check on Lianii and realized that she had a morning text from NXavier already, thanking her again for a beautiful night. She blushed and proceeded to call him first. He asked about her and Lianii and inquired about her plans for the day. Since it was a holiday the following day, and she had no work until Tuesday, Orianthi had planned to enjoy a lazy day.

She hanged up and called Mia, who informed her that Lianii was going to a movie with Mia and her daughter later and will sleepover. She chuckled at the news but was quite grateful to have a day to herself. She jumped out of bed and headed to the shower for a leisurely bath. As she stepped out of the shower, she heard the doorbell ringing incessantly.

Orianthi pulled on a robe hurriedly and run to her front door to find her Prince at the door, soaking wet from the rain. She smiled at the image he conjured in her doorway. She wondered, why didn't he say he was dropping by? Why didn't he tell he call her before he got out of the car? She ushered him into the kitchen and teased him about the ideas he was giving her neighbors, standing out there soaking wet. She took him to the guest bathroom to dry him off and found him a robe to wear while she took his damp clothing to the laundry room to dry his wet slacks and t-shirt.

She met him in the kitchen, setting out breakfast for the two of them. He thought of everything. He brought over some hot chocolate tea, French baguettes, (her favorite) whipped butter, soft brie, Canadian bacon, cherries, strawberries, grapes, and smoked turkey along with some pastries. He had enough food to feed her for days. Smiled at how domesticated he looked in a robe in her kitchen. She walked over to hug him and completely forgot she was still in a bathrobe naked underneath until she was in his embrace. He kissed her forehead and looked down at her freshly scrubbed face. She was prettier with no make-up, NXavier thought before he lowered his lips to hers. She enjoyed his kisses, and before long, he lifted and placed her on the kitchen counter to ravish her irresistible body.

As NXavier spread her thighs to fit himself between her legs, he realized she was naked. He laid her on her back to assess his damage the previous night. She felt a bit embarrassed because it was 9:00 am in the brightly lit kitchen. She motioned at the windows, and he walked over to close the windows and draw the curtains. He walked back to her and picked up the bottle of honey on the table. He opened her thighs again and brought his tongue to taste glistening lips still swollen from the night before. He apologized for hurting her, and she blushed to know that she enjoyed every second of her innermost prodding. She shivered when his tongue flicked across her knob. Her knob stiffened as he licked and suck its soft peak. He touched the inside of Her folds enticingly as she opened her legs wide enough to welcome his pleasure.

He straightened up, grabbed and poured the cold honey over her honeycomb, and proceeded to lick up every drop. The moans emanating from her were distracting. He licked then pushed the tip of his tongue into her bruise opening. The feel of his tongue expertly navigating around in her haven was soothing, relaxing, and mind-blowing. She held the back of head firmly into her snatch, enjoying the pleasure while her thighs tightening around his head. He brought her hip off the counter and held her firm cheeks in his hands. NXavier opened her legs wider as his beard, though short, brushed over her tender folds as he licked on her quivering clitoris. Orianthi screamed as she felt his long finger pushing into her heated furnace. The orgasm that followed left her weak and thirsty.

He sucks out every drop of her squirting nectar hungrily as she laid on the counter spent. NXavier closed her heated vault, assisted her to a chair at the table, and offered her a cold drink. He prepared breakfast for them both and fed her patiently. He knew that he wanted more but wanted to eat and rest first. With Lianii being out all day, he had sufficient time to make her scream over and over later. NXavier loved to hear her moan, he enjoyed watching her body stiffen in the throes of her orgasm. He was grateful that he had such a powerful effect on her to take her to the point of such a massive orgasm. He should never take her love for granted because he is at his happiest, making love to her.

After breakfast, Orianthi started to tidy up, and NXavier wanted to help, but she didn't allow him to. He risked pneumonia, taking breakfast to her on a rainy Sunday morning. He had done so much, she felt obligated to do her part. He stood behind her, wrapped his arms around her, and nibbled at her neck as she tidied up the dishes. He kept her company though distractingly while she worked and released her when she was ready to rinse and dry the dishes despite her protests. Once they were done, they walked out onto the balcony for one of their favorite past times. Watching the rain was so relaxing.

They walked back in, debating on what to do next since they were spending a full day together. Orianthi was felt comfortable with him at her home knowing that that the place was spotless, having cleaned her entire house the previous day to rest on the holiday. NXavier observed her décor and admired the design of her home. She had various pieces of furniture, though eclectic, adorning her fabulous home. He loved how inviting and cozy her home was compared to his two homes. NXavier sat on the sofa still in the bathrobe and beckoned her to join him. Orianthi sat between his long, firm legs and rested her back on his chest with his arms around her while they scanned the television for a show that they both could enjoy. She introduced him to her favorite show, "Gilmore Girls" on Netflix. He had never seen it before but heard her referring to particular quotes from the show in their numerous conversations. He wanted to get a glimpse of her world and thought process, so they binged-watched episodes all day.

They took breaks to make quick calls to their respective children and returned to watching the show. He had lots of questions about Mia and Lianii and felt a tinge of guilt, thinking that she was unable to spend time with her daughter while he was at her house. She reassured him that Mia had a daughter who was the same age as Lianii and that they were inseparable; they planned a sleepover which worked left her free to be with him. The two kids would either spend time at her house or at Mia's home. She informed him that Mia had plans to be out of town the following weekend – the same weekend he planned to visit his sons and that she would have both kids at her house. The rain persisted all day along with lightning accompanied by thunder, which encouraged the lazy day they were having. The lovers must have dozed off at some point comfortably in each other's arms.

They were awakened by a loud clap of thunder, and Orianthi turned around in NXavier arms to face him as he kissed her, and they slept some more. At some point, oblivious of time, they woke up in search of something to eat. They settled for some fruits and cheese and mimosas for a snack. As they ate, they agreed on playing a vigorous Derrick Jaxn card game. It was such a beautiful day for Orianthi, who is usually void of the adult company since her divorce. NXavier was enjoying every lazy second with her. NXavier felt having someone finally to fill the void which exists between Jocelyne, and himself was priceless. He expected to meet someone to talk to, not in his wildest dreams did he expect to find this Goddess, someone to play with, to kiss, to love but importantly to stir such deep feelings in him. Being around Orianthi was magical.

He wanted to know everything about her, her likes, her fantasies, her dreams. The card games were quite enlightening as they used the opportunity to get acquainted with each other on a different level. They maintained in-depth conversations all day long, and Orianthi could not believe how attentive he was to her every word. They prepared dinner together before taking a long, seductive shower together. He loved that she had a Jacuzzi in her bathroom and envisioned dipping in the bubbling waters with Orianthi. Now they were both in her shower, both bodies wet while they glided their slippery soapy bodies against each other. NXavier could not believe how lucky was he to have found someone so remarkable to love. He gazed at her body lovingly and kissed her to remind her of how deeply he felt for her. His fingers caressed her ample globes, her back, and her buttocks. She looked up into his eyes and got lost in those green eyes over and over again. She moaned loudly as his fingers moved to her inner thighs. She could not resist his touch. He forced her legs apart to expertly lather her secret sanctuary. Orianthi felt shy at first but began to enjoy his hands all over her body so intimately.

NXavier had never felt this way about anyone before, not even her past husband. She admired his lithe, muscular, naked body like he was a lived Michelangelo statue. They were seeing each other entirely nude for the first time, and they were both fine human specimens. Orianthi lathered NXavier's panther-like physic as thoroughly as he did hers living no stones unturned. She felt extremely horny as she pulled back his foreskin to clean his erected member. She went down on her knees to bury his entire shaft into her mouth. He held her head for support as she continued to lick his throbbing manhood while gently squeezing at his nuts. He loves the feel of her warm lips around him. He enjoys how she can take his length to her throat without gagging. She licked his nuts and placed both in her mouth as she 'wanked' his pulsating tool. He wanted this scene to stop. She returned his aching pistol to her mouth and proceed to suck the life out of him while he held on to her head to steady himself.

Chapter 8

DESIRES REVEALED

Orianthi left NXavier weakened and drained, he watched in amazement as she swallowed his essence. NXavier was tempted to bend her over and take her right there, but she whispered "later," and he obliged. He rinsed her off thoroughly and dried her body as she wiped his skin. She handed him another robe as she slipped into a sexy fuchsia, two-piece by SavagexFenty (Rihanna), which accentuates her curves and left nothing to the imagination. They dined leisurely on delicious seafood dinner that they collaborated on earlier and sipped on a glass of sweet port wine. They enjoyed each other's company. While eating, they discussed their favorite meals, travels, she regaled him about her many cruises and her desire to make love on a cruise ship. She also explained her dream of visiting Venice, Switzerland, and France. NXavier promised he would take her on a trip to Europe at some point.

He wished he could take her to Quebec as well, but that would be too risky as he could not fly to Quebec and not see his sons. He just could not jeopardize losing Orianthi to the truth. Not now, not ever, he thought. He was so deep in thoughts that she asked him where he had escaped too. He lied and said he just imagined how lovely it would be to escort her on a European trip. NXavier could hardly wait to take her on vacation with him. He wondered if he should risk introducing Orianthi to his family. What if someone asked about Jocelyne and tell Orianthi the truth. He would risk it because his mom needs to know that he finally found love. After dinner, they dimmed the lights and lit some candles in the living room as well as in her bedroom, giving both places a romantic glow similar to a secluded night club. Before bed, they chose their favorite songs to dance to. He selected slow, zouk, and every song chosen was her favorite. She enjoyed all of them. She wanted various Caribbean Calypsos, Soca, Kassav, and Reggae, songs that she loves. It became a fusion of their culture in songs.

She taught him how to dance to her songs, and he never shies at attempting, although he expressed, however, that he preferred dancing to his Zouks to her Calypsos and Socas. Orianthi relished being in his capable arms and loved being held by him. She observed the delicate way he caressed her as they danced, and thought, he is so gentle. NXavier savored how her body moved sensually to the music and valued the feel of her body on his and in his arms. It felt quite intoxicating to have her so close to him. He admired the way her nipples would pop through her bra when she was turned on, and the alluring straps linking the heart-shaped design that held the back of her panty. He had a full view of beautiful, seductive wear through her nightgown. He could hardly wait to peel that erogenous number off her curvaceous body later. He wanted her over and over again and was never satiated. In the meantime, he gazed at her in her captivating two-piece negligee. She knew he could dance, but dancing with NXavier tonight in a sexy nightgown while he lured at her was exciting. She could see his eyes glazing all over. She could feel his bump getting larger.

She loved the way he pressed her to his firm body to feel him. This made her nerve endings craved to explore more of him, inside of her, kissing her all over. She wanted him, wanted to taste his essence, wanted to feel him buried in her. NXavier craved to kiss her, desired to escape in a world where only the two of them existed. He chose a sensuous number that they both loved and pulled her into his arms. NXavier wrapped her arms around his neck as he kissed her neck and brought his lips down to her while dancing. They made their way to her bedroom and took the music along.

He was stunned to realize how expertly she decorated her room. The room was white from floor to ceiling, even the candles were white. Her bed, a California King, appeared to study with very intricate designs on the headboard. The Egyptian cotton sheets and pillowcases on her bed felt soft to the touch, the soft down comforter floated around her caramel skin like a cloud. The room accentuated her beauty. It was a perfect chamber for a Goddess like Orianthi. NXavier took their drinks, placed them on the nightstand, and walked over to her. He slipped the gown off her smoothed brown shoulders, kissing her bare skin. NXavier glanced at the sexy ensemble on her satin skin. She was perfect, he thought. He ushered her to the fluffy bed and laid her on the edge of her soft bed.

Orianthi laid naked and just licked her lips in anticipation of tasting his skin. She was aching to kiss him. She was at the very edge of the bed and could feel his finger opening her softness. Her body ached from wanting his finger inside her, but he is in no hurry. He touched her moist clit lightly, and she felt her entire body quiver. She had more nerve endings today than she thought she had and begged him to take her. He wanted her as much as she wanted him, and even more. NXavier proceeded to insert a finger slowly into her slippery crevice and felt her body writhe beneath his finger, he was shocked at how wet she was. She felt a jolt of electricity shoot through her body as she moaned and licked her dry lips. His warm tongue quickly replaced his finger, and at this point, she was not sure if he was torturing her or being patient with her. NXavier licked and sucked at her folds enthusiastically. Her lips are so soft and succulent, NXavier thought as she pushes her body towards his artful tongue and begged of him to take her. He again ignored her demands and played with her soft, tender breast, sucking her ravenously as he squeezed her tortured nipples. Her body ached to have him fill her hole. The thunder was much closer now and louder, which matched the rhythm of her hips as she pressed her cunt on his tongue and begged him to fill her. Suddenly the rain started again, and she wanted his hard shaft to replace his tongue. This time he obliged and craved to fill her with his engorged pole, yes he was ready to feel her wetness.

Orianthi went on all fours before him and waited for him to enter her tightness. She felt his finger inside her as his thumb massaged her backdoor. She could feel her juice dripping down her thighs. Her body froze, expecting the pain that accompanies such intrusion, she was in ecstasy when his knob entered her inner space. He was deep inside of her as she screamed in pain and pleasure. He stopped to asked if she was okay before he continued. Yes, he was in with a great view of her firm butt, inviting him to cream her. Yes, he was in paradise once more. This experience was better than the night before. What sweetness, sweeter than the honey episode earlier, he thought as his deep thrusts rocked her body. NXavier wished that he could spend a lifetime inside of her heated haven, and she would gladly let him if it were possible. He pulled his rod out slowly only a second as he entered again roughly to match the thunder they both loved over and over again. She was enjoying how his hard member filled her wet folds so wholly.

She tightened her muscle around his hard pole and could feel his pace increasing, feeling his fingers pressing into her hips as she pushed back on him, welcoming his hard shaft. With one final thrust, they both collapsed in a well-spent euphoric climax. He was still embedded inside her, fully erected as her insatiable muscles continued to pulsate around his massive tool, indicating she needed more of him. NXavier was eager to please; he could not have enough of her. He flipped her over onto her back and placed her feet onto his shoulders. He could see his juices dripping from her moist opening, her lips more swollen than this morning. He pushed his long finger inside her resort and spread his warm cream unto her stomach while he stared at her lips. NXavier ached to taste her lips and nipples and opened her fold to allow more of his juices to drain from her wet opening.

He admired her lubricated folds, and he could hardly wait to fill her with another load of his essence. He slowly entered her and held her globes with his long fingers and suck at each of her nipples greedily. The sensation soaring through her was heavenly, his dick felt much bigger than the previous intrusion as she felt her pussy tightened around him. He hungrily kissed her face, her forehead, neck, her cheeks until he finally brought his lips to hers. She traced his chiseled face with her fingertips and kissed his lips, his tongue pushes passed her lips and seek her tongue. She couldn't concentrate between his invasion of her mouth, and his hard shaft thrusting into her welcoming snatch, she was in heaven. She was amazed by how her body opened to him and could feel her muscle gripping him.

She felt empty every time he pulled out. NXavier felt like he was in heaven as she pushed him onto the bed and straddled him.

Orianthi stilled herself as she attempted to accommodate his 90 angle mammoth length into her dripping hot crevice. He grabbed her cheeks and open them to guide his massive rod into her soft folds as her vertical position drained her juices down his pole to moisten the knob for penetration. She finally got the knob in, and he hungrily thrust his hard rod into her soft haven. He held her butt to guide her thrust unto his impaling member to avoid hurting her though he wanted to fill her up. Once her folds fitted around his entire shaft, she increased the pace of her ride to synchronize with his breathing and slowed down every time he was at his breaking point. She wanted to make him wait as long as possible, so she lowered her body to kiss him, savoring how sweet he tasted on her tongue, deep inside her. She could feel her nipples resting on his hard chest and felt his fingers massaging the nipples.

She straightened up to continue her ride on his hard tool, cupped her massive globes as she rode him, stared at him, and brought both of her nipples up to her lips and sucked at them enticingly. She quickened her paced as an orgasm rocked her entire body over him. She laid still over him for a second to regain her composure while he thrust into her stilled body. The site of her sucking her nipples, her powerful orgasm, and the tightening of her muscles around his pole was too much for him to bear. He groaned raucously as his powerful tool became much larger inside her than before, which resulted in him shooting another load of his juices in her heated pool one more time. She kissed his soft lips and laid lifeless in his arms.

They slept in each other arms for hours and were awaked by a huge clap of thunder overhead. NXavier limped out of bed to the kitchen naked, and Orianthi ogled through sleepy eyes at NXavier as he walked away. She admired his panther-like prowess, which emanated in each step. He returned with a plate of assorted fruits, two glasses of wine on a tray, and two chilled bottles of water. How did he know she was thirsty? She wondered. She got of bed and straightened the sheets as he observed her naked body bent over to make the bed; his bulk hardened from the site. He could not believe he still wanted her. How was this humanly possible? He wrapped his robe around his naked body and walked to the next room to speak to his son, while she checked with Mia about Lianii. Mia knew that NXavier was at her house and had played interference all day with Lianii, she would wait for the next day to get the juicy details about her day, she told her as much. She smiled as she hanged up the phone and turn to see him staring at her from the doorway teasingly.

She reached out a hand to him, and he followed her to her shower. He got an instant erection as he saw the Jacuzzi bubbling. She went back to the room to get their drinks, fruits, towels and lit some scented candles. They rinsed out in the shower and stepped into the heated bubbles of the Jacuzzi. The heated water massages her sore garden, and he pulled her close to him to rub her shoulders playfully. He continues to her breast, then his fingers found her epicenter and inserted a finger into her painful rose. She moaned painfully as the bubbles vibrated on her flower. NXavier saw the painful expression on her face. He lifted her body and placed her on the edge of the tub and opened her thighs as the heated water bathe her soreness. NXavier opened her legs and watched her swollen lips in the bubbling water and longed to feel her on his tongue. He placed her on the edge of the tub and brought his hot lips down to her opening as he massaged her softness lovingly with his tongue. She looked down at his head and run her fingers through his wet curls and closed her eyes to allow her body to respond to the taste of his expert tongue on her folds.

The more he licked her sore opening, the more she wanted him and begged him to fill her up. The sound of Orianthi's voice pleading with him made his pulsating pole harder. He pulled her up and lowered her back into the water as he handed her a drink. His stiff pole was in view when he stretched to get their drinks, she lowered herself into the tub to fit her lips around his engorged member. He could not resist as his body betrayed him by responding pleasurably to her lips on his wood. NXavier knows that he was in love with Orianthi, but he could swear he loved her more every time she sucked his rod, and the feel of the tip hitting the back of her throat. She had art for this sucking, he thought as she sucked on his soft sacks below his throbbing shaft. She pulled down his foreskin and hungrily sucked him until he erupted in her mouth forcefully. He watched as some of his creams slipped down her chin, he wiped the creamed off and bent to capture her lips into a deep kiss.

They laid in the tub lazily, as he fed her some fruits. They sipped at their wine and talked about their plans for the week. NXavier told her about the boys and his scheduled trip back home the following weekend. He wondered which night she was free to come over for dinner. He felt a pinged of guilt bringing her to his home knowing Jocelyne had shared his bed there, though never intimately. He needed to create some memories with her at his house. They agreed to take Thursday off to spend the day together at his home before his trip on Friday. NXavier was already mentally planning on what he could do to top what they had done before. He loved this girl to distraction and will spend the rest of his life, showing her how much she meant to him. He wiped the water off her face and leaned over to kiss her as she massaged his semi erected bulge. His kisses deepened, and it was not long before NXavier brought Orianthi back onto his thighs to straddle him once more.

Chapter 9

A Day in the Clouds

On Thursday, Orianthi got exquisitely dressed for her day with NXavier. He did not divulge the plans for the day to her, despite having pleaded with him all week. She had seen him once since he left her home the Sunday morning. He stopped at her job to bring her lunch as an excuse to see her on Tuesday. She loves the thoughtful ways he dots on her. He continued to send her hallmark cards and deliver her meals on the days she worked. Today they both were off, Lianii left early for a field trip, and she had the sitter scheduled to come in after school to be with the kids. She was ready for his secret plans, whatever they were. He picked her up at 7:46 am, escorted her to the car after a quick hug and a soft kiss on her forehead. He couldn't trust himself to kiss her lips. That's the most he could muster before he lost all will power and dragged back in to make passionate love to her all day.

He walked her to her side, opened her door, and helped her into the truck. He enjoyed helping her in an out of his vehicle, it always reminded him of their first meeting. He began driving but refused to divulge where they were going, so she stopped asking and relaxed. He drove with his left hand as his right hand held on to hers. She admired how he effortlessly maneuver this truck with one hand. They talked about the children, work, his upcoming trip to Quebec, and her weekend plans with the two girls. He wondered when she would introduce him to Mia, Lorelai, and the girls. They obviously are her best friends and family, but she has never offered, which meant she was not prepared to share her full life with him. He asked her about her reluctance to introduce him previously, and she that she would, in time, so he decided not to force the issue.

They drove for twenty-five minutes until he pulled into the parking lot of Lockheed Martin, it was beautiful. He was taking her to his workplace. She was excited! Before meeting him, she knew nothing about Lockheed Martin, but now Orianthi was almost an expert as he spoke to her regularly about his work, and on the days he did not, she became quite inquisitive. He secured her necessary clearance to access the building and gave her a private tour of the magnificent building. He was amazed by how intrigued she was in his world. He answered her many questions and introduced her to his coworkers. Some of his colleagues mistook Orianthi for his wife, and he failed to correct them, which made her wonder if he had not discussed his divorce with them. After the tour was over, he took her to his office, where he had a delicious breakfast waiting.

Orianthi was surprised to see that he had a picture of Jocelyne and the boys as well as a beautiful pic of her on his desk. She blushed at the thought of him publicly displaying her or him staring at her picture while he works. She loved the view from his window. NXavier came and stood directly behind her pointing out the different landmarks. His arms wrapped around her. She nestled in his arms and enjoyed the view. He took her to the table set for two in a corner in his office, for breakfast. They fed each other, and talk a lover breakfast like they were in a secluded restaurant. After breakfast, she thanks him for a really romantic affair in an unusual setting. NXavier left the cleaning crew a note and an enormous tip, he secured the documents he required for the weekend and left.

Orianthi and NXavier spent the rest of the day sightseeing all of his favorite places. He took her to The Philip and Patricia Frost Museum of Science in Miami, and she was able to identify having watched all the seasons of The Big Bang Theory; otherwise, she would have been lost. She was quite fascinated by the futuristic features displayed. She fell in love with him all over again when he spent the better part of the tour explaining each prototype to her. Before this she was intrigued by his brilliance, now she was convinced he was genius. He was a genius who was in love with her. She blushed at the thought. He took her to some high-end boutiques for shopping and bought her a few pricy outfits, shoes, and some jewelry despite her protests. They stopped at a Japanese restaurant boasting the best seafood for lunch and had sushi.

NXavier took Orianthi to the Lion Country Safari, she had seen the advertisement on television but never visited. Lion Country Safari is a scenic drive-in route through an exotic zoo in West Palm Beach, Florida. Some animals she had seen before in a regular zoo, but most of the animals were seen on Animal Planet or the Discovery Channel. He became her personal tour guide as they drove at two miles per hour through the 7-mile course. At some point, they became stranded as a rhinoceros or zebra chose this inopportune time to cross the road. She took many pictures to share with her daughter and friends. She saw peacocks, lions, panthers, pythons, giraffes, baboons, and many animals to remember without the accompanying booklet provided. It was an enchanting tour, and she could not wait to bring the girls back this weekend, they would love it.

They were both exhausted as they left the safari, and NXavier finally headed to his home. He had an exquisite home that matched her mental image of his house. She loved it, much bigger than her home, but he has two boys to her one daughter. NXavier gave her a tour of his marvelous home and escorted her to a beautiful room with a private bath and brought in her shopping bags, and placed them on the bed. Orianthi undressed and headed to the shower. Orianthi emerged from the bathroom in one of his t-shirts and laid in the soft, comfortable bed. He knocked on the door, and when he got no response, he opened the bedroom door and found her fast asleep. He was a bit disappointed but thought a nap may be required because he needed her rested for the night ahead. He took some pictures of her sleeping face for keepsake while he is away from her.

Afterward, he went for a shower and selected his outfit for the night. He called his boys, 'sans' Jocelyne, who had pretty much avoided him as much as possible since she told him about her feelings towards him. She had conveniently been scared for every visit, and he had just enjoyed being a dad without the strain. He was happy, and the woman in the next room was the source of his newfound happiness. He had no intention of wasting a second worrying about Jocelyne's disappearance. Orianthi woke up around six pm and went in search of NXavier who was dosing off on the chair peacefully; it was a shame to wake him up, she thought. She took some pictures of him for the weekend and turned to walk back in the room when his hands grabbed onto her and pulled her down on him. He whispered, "hello," she whispered, "hi."

He kissed her forehead and asked what she wanted for dinner.

She settled for a delicious smoothie, and he joined her in one as they sat at the kitchen table talking. NXavier continuously checked the time, which made her wonder if he had somewhere to be. Once they were done with their smoothies, he asked her to get dressed as he had a surprise for her. She chose a multi-colored, spaghetti strap romper paired it off with a short orange jeans jacket and an orange Lace-Up Hollow Knot Peep Toe Platform Wedges with an orange cross over bag he bought for her earlier. When Orianthi walked out to him, he was speechless. NXavier knew that Orianthi is a stunning woman, but he thought she got prettier every time he saw her. He took some pictures of her as she admired this tall, lithe man in form-fitting jeans and royal shirt, opened at the neck revealing some curly chest hairs. It is amazing how he looked excellent in whatever he wore. She loved to see him in everything he wore. She wished she could kiss his chest right now, but they were dressed and ready. If she touches him for any reason, they would never leave the house.

He drove her to a live concert at a music festival in West Palm Beach featuring all her favorite female artists. The lineup included: Evanescence, Jewel, Dixie Chicks, Sarah McLachlan, Avil Lavinge, HER, Heart, Leela James, Norah Jones, Jessica Simpson, Tamar, Toni Braxton, Alanis Moricette, and Lauryn Hill. If she did not love him before now, she was sure to fall madly in love with him after seeing this line-up. Orianthi hugged him and gave him a huge kiss to show her appreciation. She wished her friends Mia and Lorelai were here, at least Mia. Those were her best friends' favorite artists too. She promised mentally to record the show for them. The concert was an outdoor event, where the guests were seated facing the stage on blankets. He checked his phone for a message and immediately had a contented look on his face. She wondered who he was busy texting, it seems a bit suspicious, so unlike him, but she let it go.

NXavier escorted Orianthi to their VIP seats closer to the stage. She was so excited about his latest surprise that she was eager to sit. Unfortunately, the two empty seats left were not next to each other, NXavier was not seated next to her, flagged the sides of her seat were Mia and Lorelei!

How did they get here??

She stared at them in amazement as they eagerly filled her in about NXavier's role in getting them here to be with her. He heard them talking about the concert on the phone several months ago, and got her friends' numbers off her phone and invited them as a surprise. She reached over Mia to squeeze his hand and introduced him to her girlfriends. She inquired about Zainii, and Mia told her that both girls were at her home with the sitter. She hugged her friends and exchange seats with Mia to sit next to her Prince. NXavier offered to get their drinks, and she tagged along because she needed to thank him again for her surprise. How were her friends able to keep such an immense secret from her? She could not have loved him more than she did at this point.

While they waited on their drinks, she walked into his arms, pull his face down to her lips and kissing him deeply. He held her in his arms, enjoying her closeness, but he reminded her that the concert will start soon. He extracted himself from her reluctantly and paid for their drinks and located their seats just as the announcer walked on stage to announce the first act. From the first artist to the very last performance, the ladies were on their feet, singing away. Although he only heard of the songs on her playlist before, he was stunned that they knew the lyrics to all the songs. NXavier was amazed at them and happy that Orianthi stood in front of him with his arms around her shoulders as they swayed to the music.

Every love song was romantic when Jewel sang, "You were meant for me," the song touched a raw nerve in him. NXavier looked down at her angelic face and was pleased he had her, was delighted to be with her, and knew that she was made for him. He barely felt guilty about not telling her about Jocelyne. He was pleased to be hers. It was a fabulous concert; the ladies were beside themselves, talking up a storm in the car as he drove them home. He was finally happy to see Orianthi in her niche, she was the same with them, confident, witty, down to earth, and beautiful. Orianthi glanced at him, and he seemed lost in thoughts, so she turned the conversations over to him, which may not have been a good idea because now the girls wanted to know all about his intentions for Orianthi. They thanked him again for a beautiful surprise and loved how happy he made their friend, and each one sternly cautioned him to keep it up before they exited the car at their respective homes.

Finally, he was alone with her, though he loved hearing the chatter among the three he loves time alone with his princess. He will be gone until Tuesday, and anytime with Orianthi was precious. He pulled into the driveway, knowing that her sitter was home with the kids. He wished that he could drive to his home and place her back in one of his shirts, she looked gorgeous in his t-shirt earlier. He reached for her hand and kissed it, then press her hand to his cheek. He will miss her in the next few days. She has become an essential part of him. He pulled her towards him and kissed her senselessly. Afterward, he released her and exited the car, he collected her shopping bags out of the trunk and escorted her to her door. When they got to the door, he whispered how much he hated being away from her and how unsafe she was standing here with him. It took all his will power not to ravish her right there. She kissed his neck as he held her and calmed his raging need for her. NXavier kissed her forehead, hugged her a little tighter than usual, lowered his lips to her one last time before he disappeared into the dark night.

Chapter 10

KNIGHT TO THE RESCUE, PART 1

Orianthi arrived home and placed her packages in her room, then she checked on the girls and sitter and hurriedly showered for bed. As she got into her room, she retrieved her phone and called NXavier, who was still driving home. She loves keeping him company on the phone on long trips. They spoke to each other until he was safely in bed. She was awakened at 6:20 am by NXavier, who was on his way to the airport for his scheduled flight. She hated him on a plane. Although the trip from Fort Lauderdale airport to Quebec's was roughly less than 5 hours, it always felt like an eternity to both of them because they could not communicate with each other during that time. At least she was working until 6:30pm today, and the distraction was welcomed. She prayed for his safety as she got ready for work. The girls would be going to school later, but the sitter would stay on until she returned home. She would surprise the girls with trips to the Sci-Fi Museum in Miami and the Lion Country Safari this weekend before their journey to St Lucia.

♡~♡~♡~♡~♡~♡~♡~♡~♡~♡~♡

NXavier boarded the airline and started working on the document he carried along with him. He was engrossed in work when colossal turbulences nearly threw his hot coffee on his thigh. The turbulences got much worse as the pilot apologized for the rough flight, requested that everyone fasten their seatbelts and attempt to calmly explain his plans for the plane. Then a huge sound was heard as aircraft continued to sway. The air hostesses ordered to prepare passengers for the emergency landing. He looked out through the window and saw that the area did not even seem to look like Quebec, not even remotely; however, the plane was doing an emergency landing. NXavier wondered what could be wrong to force this emergent landing and was informed that there was a crack on the glass in the cockpit of the plane. They exited the plane in Buffalo, New York, and were ushered into a shuttle and taken into a hotel. Unfortunately, in his haste, his phone fell and broke, leaving him with no contact with his loved ones.

NXavier tried to recall numbers to no avail, Orianthi was at work today, so he tried calling her a few times, but she was busy for most of the calls either in a patient's room or at a meeting. His other requests to speak to Orianthi left him on hold until he got fed up, and he hung up. The only route available was an email. So he emailed his family and Orianthi about his ordeal for the day and subsequent plans. He hated not reaching Orianthi because she will never call him or disturb him while he is with his sons but would still expect him to contact her to let her know that he landed, and he was safe. He took a different flight to Quebec later that day and arrived at 10:00 p.m. yet with no phone, no numbers on a Friday night. He came home to his sons, all excited to hear the details of his adventures. He opened his laptop to check the status of his phone replacement request and was told that the phone would be delivered on Sunday before 2:00 p.m., he could hardly wait. This did not help in decreasing his need to contact Orianthi.

He was finally home with his boys but was still worried about the no response to his many emails. He wondered what she was doing, why hadn't she checked her emails. The next day he kept himself busy with the boys to tried and forget the absence of Orianthi in his life. Jocelyne surprisingly was present with no plans of her own and entirely involved in his ideas with the boys. She tagged along to a basketball game, the movies, and dinner.

This was the first time they were out together as a family in over 3 years. He was stunned by her inclusion in their plans but remained quiet. If her coming along made his sons happier, he was all for it; they seemed so glad to have her on their dad dates.

♡♡♡♡♡♡♡♡♡♡♡♡♡♡♡♡♡♡♡♡♡♡♡♡♡

Orianthi was grateful for her busiest day ever. She regularly checked her phone for messages from NXavier to let her know that he had landed, but there was none. After work, she took the girls out to get their hair washed and styled manicures and pedicures. They loved the attention; however, she became concerned and kept checking for a message from NXavier. Later they stopped at Friday's for dinner and headed for home. Before bed, she checked again, and there was nothing from him. At that point, she began to worry, "Is he okay?" she thought. She had never called him while he visited his family for obvious reasons, as the last thing she needed was to disturb his time with his sons. She fell asleep and dreamt he got lost on his way to Quebec and, as a result, was redirected back to Florida and back to her.

The girls loved the Philip and Patricia Museum of Science. It was innovative and interactive. The girls spent the day exploring the museum and taking Snapchat pictures for their profiles and had lunch at a nearby Burger King. After leaving the museum, she took the girls to Burlington at the Sawgrass Mall for some needed summer attires. Both girls were headed to St Lucia to spend summer with their respective grandparents, and Orianthi thought getting the necessary shopping out of the way was a great idea. In fact, she was using the various expeditions to masked the fact that she had heard nothing from NXavier in over 24 hours, which was unlike him. She was worried about him tremendously. It was unlike him to spend a day without texting her even when he is in Quebec. They stopped at the food court for dinner and went home.

♡~♡~♡~♡~♡~♡~♡~♡~♡~♡~♡

NXavier had a great day with the boys, but he seemed a bit distracted, not his usual bubbly self. They all stopped for dinner on the way home, but NXavier was confused about Jocelyne's sudden interest in when he was coming back to Quebec, and when was his next vacation. NXavier was perplexed by her questions, they were not the norm from Jocelyne. He proceeded to encourage her line of questioning to explore her intentions. Jocelyne asked if it was possible to plan a trip to see his parents. He was quite puzzled at her request as has not encouraged any family interactions in the past and had not accompanied them to any of his trips to his parents with the kids; however, she now wanted to suggest a trip. NXavier stared at her to assess whether she was joking or serious. NXavier then responded that he would make inquiries of his parents on their plans and finalized the trip around his schedule. They were then distracted by the boys who started asking questions about their unplanned trip for the school break.

NXavier had a difficult time getting the boys ready for bed because all they spoke about was their trip. After the boys were tucked comfortably in bed, read to and sleepy, he went to his study and logged on to his computer, hoping to get an email from Orianthi, and there was still nothing. He missed her so much! He had lost his only lifeline to her – his phone. He missed her pictures, he missed her smiling face, her voice, her kisses. He sent her another message and log off then thought again about Jocelyne's suggestion. "What was she trying now?" he thought, he was finally happy. Did she sense he was happy and needed to destroy it? He shook his head and took a book to read along with his laptop bag with him to his room. Since their last conversation, he had been occupying another room. NXavier explained to his boys when they enquired, that he was continually working at nights to avoid disturbing their mom he needed his own bedroom.

NXavier got ready for bed and read himself to sleep. He remembered thinking of the last time he made love to Orianthi in the hot tub. He dreamt of his missing songbird that night, he casually recalled driving her home one night a few weeks ago after dancing all night sensually, and he reached over to fondle her and found no panties. He looked at her face to see a mischievous smile appearing on her sweet heart-shaped face. She apparently removed the panties just before she left for the car. He was startled as she undid his button for his cotton slacks and unzip his pants and continue to massage his erect member while he drove. He is an excellent driver, but feeling her finger massage his shaft sent chills up his entire body. It was challenging to navigate the road but enjoyed this experience as she removed her seatbelt and bent over to take his full member into her mouth. He had just enough willpower to pull over to the curb as she sucked on his engorged phallus. He erupted into her mouth the seconds the car rolled on the curb. He screamed out her name in ecstasy and rested in his seat to regain his composure. Orianthi expertly sucked and swallowed every drop of his juices to avoid soiling the car, then sat up as if nothing happened and turn the radio on to an Ellie Golden Pandora playlist singing along to Ellie's "How Long Will I Love You."

They drove home to her beautiful voice serenading him, NXavier knew that without a shadow of a doubt that he loved this woman and would find a way to keep her in his arms forever. NXavier had a very restless night afterward. Little did he know that Jocelyne came to his room to ask if he was interested in a nightcap and heard him moaning and screaming Orianthi's name in the throes of ecstasy. Jocelyne returned to her room, quite conflicted. Who is Orianthi? Why was NXavier screaming out her name while he masturbates? She knew that he did, had heard him pleasure himself before in the shower; however, this instance sounded different. She felt a ping of jealousy as she laid in bed that night. She had no desire for him sexually but made the decision not to allow someone else to replace her. She decided to investigate who this Orianthi was to assess if his interest in her was a threat to her.

♡♡♡♡♡♡♡♡♡♡♡♡♡♡♡♡♡♡♡♡♡♡

The following day was dark and gloomy for Orianthi. She barely had an hour of rest the previous night thinking of various scenarios as to why she had not heard from NXavier. Was he sick? Are his boys sick? The dream about him getting lost frazzled her. She missed him tremendously. One thing for sure was that NXavier›s absence left a vast void in her that only he can fill. She tried to get out of bed and fell sore all over. She had a sore throat, eyes puffy and stinging, body aches, and a dry cough. To top it off, she might have to cancel the drive to The Lion Country Safari with the girls because of the weather. Orianthi realized that there was no way she would be able to drive in her present condition. She walked in to check on the girls and found them asleep on the sofas in front of the TV in the den, probably worn out from the activities of the previous day. Orianthi thought if she were getting the flu, it would be best for Mia to collect the girls as she did not want to expose them to the virus before their scheduled trip.

She proceeded to call Mia, who gladly agreed to pick up her goddaughter and her niece since Lorelei was still out of town until Tuesday. She quickly packed a bag for the girls, got their outfits and travel documents ready for Mia, and quarantine herself in her room until they left. She had a shower, made a cup of hot Theraflu tea, took some Dayquil, and went back to bed. She woke up later in a cold sweat, she was shivering, head throbbing, throat sore, coughing profusely. She grabbed her phone to see if she had any messages from NXavier, and there were no text messages, but Orianthi realized she had notifications of at least 15 letters, which seems excessive for a weekend. She ignored them went in search of some tea, more Dayquil, and another shower.

She returned to bed feeling worse now, her head was throbbing profusely, she was feverish, had a non-productive cough, and the sore throat persisted. She prepared a double dose of tea, popped in 1000 mgs of vitamin C into her mouth and chew the tablets, and drank some more tea. Orianthi sent a message to Lorelei and Mia about her status and turned on the Hallmark Channel to escape into a love story before silencing her phone since the ringing made her headache worse. She eventually dozed off and woke up at 5:50 p.m. with a 102.5° fever and chills, nausea, the was headache worst and now accompanied by right lower quadrant pain. Wow, she thought, she needed professional help. She got dressed and decided to go to the emergency room at her job. She decided to text the girls on the ride over and uber herself to the Emergency Room, forgetting that she had silenced her phone.

♡~♡~♡~♡~♡~♡~♡~♡~♡~♡~♡

NXavier noticed a change in Jocelyne immediately when he walked out of his room that morning. She was abrupt, distant, aloof, and was already dressed for breakfast with her friends instead of Sunday breakfast at home with him and the boys. NXavier tried to engage her in a conversation, but she had retreated to her previous distant, monosyllabic answers. He ignored her and walked to his study to check his emails, still no response from Orianthi. He could hardly wait for his phone to arrive to check up on Orianthi, she had the girls for the weekend. He was sitting at his desk, wondering how tired Orianthi must be running all over the enormous Mall with those girls. NXavier sent her another email, then called his mom the confirm their visit at the end of the month. His mom was not too happy upon hearing Jocelyne would be coming, but she agreed to accommodate her daughter-in-law only because she can get to see her two boys. He checked his upcoming vacation and bought their tickets.

He hated planning a vacation without discussing it with Orianthi. So he decided right there and then to surprise Orianthi with tickets to Martinique for the July 4th weekend

Before his trip to France as it would not impact her too much. He continued to work for three more hours until the boys swam his office, wondering what he had planned for them for the day. After breakfast, NXavier took them to get their haircuts, then took them shopping for their trip to France. He must remember to keep it low key to avoid a repeat of last night incessant questions. They went to a water park and spent the rest of the morning, enjoying their time with their dad. NXavier was grateful for the day's adventures because they kept his mind off his Orianthi. He still felt deflated without access to her even with all the questions, jokes, laughter, and rabblerousing with the boys. On the way home, NXavier stopped for a late lunch at Red Lobster and took home a meal for Jocelyne.

When they arrived home, Jocelyne was somewhere inside. As he entered his study, he saw Jocelyne getting off his computer and was surprised to see her as she would never venture in there. She has her personal laptop and printer set up in her powder room and had no reason to be in his study. The only time she would visit his study was to talk to him or retrieved the boys but never at his desk or on his laptop. Because of the classified documents in there, no one was allowed in his research without his supervision, and Jocelyne knew that. Jocelyne was still her usual stoical demeanor, again NXavier ignored her coldness and proceed to tell her about the dates for their weeklong trip so she could note in the planner on her phone. He then informed her of their activities for the day, how the boys were currently in the shower and that they brought her a meal from Red Lobster. He asked her if his phone had been delivered, and Jocelyne pointed to the parcel on his desk and walked out sullenly.

NXavier activated his phone and downloaded his contact list while he checked his emails, still no messages from Orianthi. At that point, he began to get even more worried. Once his phone was activated and working, he downloaded WhatsApp and send her a message. When she is home, her phone is always within reach, so where could she be? He thought. Was there something wrong with her or the girls? He texted her again on WhatsApp, still no response, so he began to get frantic and proceeded to call her, but there was no answer from her. NXavier was beside himself. Was she angry with him? It's Sunday; maybe she was with Mia, so he texted Mia. Mia informed him that Orianthi had the flu, and she had taken the girls from her. In her last text, she said that she was heading to bed. That was at 4:00 p.m. She put him on hold and contacted Lorelei to enquire about whether she had spoken to Orianthi, but she had the same previous text. NXavier was beside himself with anxiety.

NXavier immediately secured a red-eye flight to Florida, called the boys in and told them that he had an emergency at work and needed to fly out. NXavier also told them the dates of their upcoming trip to France to cheer them up, and informed Jocelyne that there was a work-related emergency which required his presence in Florida and that he needed to fly out that night. One look of his distraught face told her he was worried about something, but what? NXavier requested a car service to take him to the airport and got himself ready. He had dinner prepared by 7:00 p.m., his suitcase was already at the door with his laptop. They sat and had a quick dinner he read to the boys and tucked them in before his shower, although it was much too early for bed. All the time, NXavier is consumed with thoughts of Orianthi, where was she? How sick is she? Why is Orianthi not picking up her phone?

He passed Jocelyne in the hallway deep in thoughts, which made her worry that the emergency was worse than he described. NXavier had never discussed his work with her in the past because it was classified. Hence the reason his study remained locked at all times and could only be accessed with a code known only to him. At breakfast, she told her friends about his dream, and they too encouraged her to investigate. If only she could check his emails. She was shocked to realize his study was opened when she got home. She went in to see if his laptop or desktop was on, but both were off and password protected. She pretended to bring his package in his study and wondered if he had the trip itinerary printed on his desk.

She saw how shocked he was to find her in there but was too preoccupied with something to realize what it was?

Jocelyne wondered how bad the 'emergency' was and how it would impact their lives and the upcoming trip to France in three weeks. She also asked if his 'emergency' had anything to do with one "Orianthi," the named that he screamed out in his dream the night before. Why was she so jealous? He was happy, he seems content, he had never asked about her feelings again, so why was she, Jocelyne suspicious about a name in his dream. She did not want NXavier to think of her or be with her; Jocelyne, just wanted her life and sons' lives to remain unchanged. If he had any idea of running off, she would need to find a way to keep him. So until this matter is resolved, she would continue to be vigilant.

Chapter 11

Knight to the Rescue, Part 2

The Uber dropped Orianthi at the hospital, and she limped her way inside. She was triaged and ushered to bed. By then, her temperature was higher than before, and the pain to her right lower quadrant had gotten worst. She felt nauseous and wished NXavier was there with her. Why would she get sick on the one weekend he is away and had not contacted her, not once? She felt so alone, Lorelei was out for her Anniversary, the girls were with Mia, and should stay far away from her. She had blood works done, intravenous fluids hanging and were being taken to Radiology for a chest x-ray and an abdominal ultrasound.

Just after she returned to the room, the doctor confirmed her diagnosis of Bronchitis, but an ultrasound revealed that she had acute Appendicitis. She was hurriedly being prepared for emergency surgery, which was scheduled as soon as her blood results came in from the laboratory. Security was called in to secure her belongings, her bag with her silent phone and laptop. The pain was so excruciating that she never remembered to call her friends. She was comforted by the fact that she worked in the building and was known by some members of staff, and the nursing supervisor had already been down to see her.

She kept on tossing and writhing in pain as she was not given any pharmacologic pain management until surgery as once the Appendicitis pain stops, it would signify a rupture of the inflamed appendix. She felt like she was in hell and was impatient with the staff, the surgical team, and everyone else. She was very relieved to see the anesthesiologist as sedation would end the nightmare she was going through, she thought. She started counting backward and drifted off happily, running into Xavier's arms.

♡~♡~♡~♡~♡~♡~♡~♡~♡~♡~♡~♡~♡

NXavier left his home much earlier than required, he was impatient to get to Orianthi. He called Mia to asked if she had a key to the house. By then, they just assumed that her phone was dead or she was sleeping. He hated to think about her being sick in bed all alone. Why couldn't she have been ill last weekend? Now he was millions of miles away and utterly dependent on a plane to get to her. The flight left quite earlier than expected, and after he rechecked the trip, he realized it was on time and hat he read the time wrong. NXavier knew that he was in love with Orianthi; there is not one doubt in his mind that she adored him, but what would he do if something were to happen to her. He hated the lies that he had told her, and he desperately hoped that those lies would not cost him his soulmate. Why was he thinking of such when all he wanted was to run to her? He was tortured by the time he landed at 11:00 p.m. and followed the address on his GPS navigation to Mia's home. Thank God she lived in Fort Lauderdale! Mia and the girls met him at the door.

NXavier drove as fast as humanly possible and pulled in to Orianthi's driveway, bolting up her stairs two at a time, very eager to see and hug her with no care for his own health. He placed the gifts he brought her on her chair, removed his jacket, and set it on the back of the sofa and slowly open her bedroom door. To his astonishment, the room was empty, the bed looked slept in, and a cup of tea filled halfway sat on the bedside table. NXavier walked to the bathroom to look for Orianthi; she not in their either. He did a search of the entire house and realized that she was missing. He then called Mia and Lorelei to let them know. Her car was in the driveway, her home was empty, she was not answering her phone, the fear that consumed him was insurmountable. Where could she be? He paced the house until Mia arrived with the girls, and they started calling the nearby hospitals. He could not stand still, so he left them in the house and drove to her workplace, thinking maybe she had gone in to check on something at work.

His fear of something horrible could have happened to her was making him ill. He thought of calling the police, but it was too soon to make a missing person report. He came through the Emergency Room and said her name to one of the security officers who took him to her unit. When he arrived there and inquired about her, no one had seen her. The nurses informed him that Orianthi had the weekend off. He felt his heart sank and just stood there shaking. The nurses at the station asked him what was wrong, he told them how the last time he spoke with Orianthi she said that she had the flu and now it seems that she is missing. The staff felt heart heartbroken over the news and started praying that Orianthi was safe somewhere, wondering if his announcement was a mistake and started brainstorming on possible scenarios. Fortunately, the nursing supervisor came in to do her rounds in the middle of the commotion, and NXavier's relief informed him that she saw Orianthi in the Emergency Room earlier.

She made a few calls and found out that Orianthi was being transferred to the surgical unit in a few minutes. The nursing supervisor escorted him to the surgical group, and NXavier immediately called Mia to tell her the news. Mia called the sitter to stay with the girls and headed to the hospital, where the security took her up to meet NXavier. They both were in tears to know she was alone, and had surgery and told no one. A few minutes later, the nurses came in and ushered them out to prepare the bed. She was brought into the bed while the nurses' handover report and secured some lines on her. Orianthi was still groggy from the surgery and in pain. When she saw NXavier and Mia, she was relieved and apologized for not contacting them. NXavier was angry at her for not telling her friends but forgave her quickly.

When they were finally allowed in, the nurse told them they could stay with her but not for long because she may be sedated for the rest of the night. NXavier refused to leave her. He was off until Wednesday anyway, so Mia decided to head home, collect some clothes and toiletries for her and update Lorelei and the girls. NXavier sat next to her on a recliner provided by the nursing assistant, held her free hand, and bent over to kiss her. He felt the anger, fear, the anguish lifted off him like a weighted blanket. NXavier did not know he was crying until he gripped her other hand, caressing his face. She whispered his name; he nodded and kissed her again, forgetting she also had the flu. He told her he was here, and he loved her; she echoed his sentiment and drifted off to sleep. NXavier laid on the recliner and dozed off, holding on to her hand.

♡♡♡♡♡♡♡♡♡♡♡♡♡♡♡♡♡♡♡♡♡♡♡♡

Orianthi was dreaming that she was lying in a beautiful meadow, staring up at the sky under a shaded tree, she could hear a bubbling brook* nearby, and birds chirping above, the cool breeze blew around her and in the distance. She spied NXavier in the distance and called out his name. He came running to her and laid in the grass next to her, lost in each other's embrace. The pain coursing through her abdomen took her away from the meadow as she began to moan, her moans were similar to those in the throes of ecstasy that NXavier was enjoying them until her voiced said his name and she sounded like she was in pain. He opened his eyes to see her eyes still closed, but she was guarding her abdomen. He summoned the nurse with the call bell and continued to massage her arms, murmuring to her. She called out his name a few times but was oblivious to his presence in the room with her. It was painful to see Orianthi so broken, and in pain, NXavier felt helpless.

NXavier could not bear to see her in pain, he needed her to be comfortable as soon as possible and was quite impatient with the nursing staff. They medicated her, and he waited until she was asleep and rushed home for a shower and supplies. When he returned, he saw her bag, which means Mia had been in, and he was thankful that she was still asleep. She muttered his name a few times and smile, and he wondered if she would ever remember what she was thinking of now. NXavier stood at the window, drinking his coffee when he heard Orianthi whispered his name; he turned to see her eyes opened, staring at him. He rushed over because she was attempting to sit up, he reoriented her to the unit, soothe her and called for the nurses. She asked why he was in Florida so soon, and why did he leave the boys to be here? NXavier looked at her crossly and wondered if wild horses could keep him away from her surgical bedside. NXavier was grateful that no one knew Orianthi was having surgery, imagine hearing the news in Quebec, he would have been entirely devastated.

She told him how sick she felt and calling a cab to the emergency room. She remembered going for the ultrasound but remembered nothing else but running to his arms and laying in a meadow with him and waking up to him here with her. He climbed into the bed with her and just hugged her. Orianthi missed him so much, and here he was, cutting his trip short to be with her. She remembered getting the flu because she did not hear from him for a few days. He explained his unfortunate predicament with his phone and how many emails he sent her. She recalled seeing the messages before she went to the hospital but was too sick to check them out. She asked the nurse to get her belonging from security so she could read all his letters. She felt so loved reading his desperate words. Yet Orianthi felt so guilty, pulling him away from his sons though obviously, she needed him. What will happen if he has to be there with his children indefinitely? What will she do? What will become of her?

Orianthi felt the tears roll down her cheeks, throbbing pulsating behind her eyelids. Orianthi was so relieved that NXavier was here with her instead of Quebec. He realized she was crying and asked if she was in pain; she nodded yes, although it was the furthest from the truth. He turned her over and kiss her forehead and held her to him, thinking of his anguish of not knowing if she was hurt, kidnapped, or dead the night before. At least she is safe now, in his arms where she belongs. He wished he had never left her side now or ever. She wrapped her arms around his massive, muscular shoulders, rest her head on his chest and sob herself to sleep as he kissed away her tears, her pain, her loneliness. She was in his arms the only place she wished to be.

Orianthi remained at the hospital for 2 more days with her family taking turns to care for her. Mia brought the girls in a few times to assure them she was okay. Lorelei flew back home to help, but NXavier only left to get her flowers, books, her favorite foods when her diet was advance to regular meals and other miscellaneous items. The girls went to St Lucia on Tuesday morning as scheduled, and Orianthi hated not seeing them off, but she always had Mia and Lorelei as backup parents and never had to worry about Lianii if she is with either one of them. Orianthi was extremely grateful for the bond she has with her best friends and support system that they have developed for each other away from their home of St Lucia, where their extended families reside.

She was discharged on Wednesday morning and driven home by NXavier. Her apartment was spotless when she arrived, much different than she had left it on Sunday evening. NXavier had gotten a professional service over to clean, do the laundry, and had overnight soft Egyptian Cotton sheets and a new down comforter for her in her favorite colors, peridot green and yellow. She thought he overdid it with the flowers at the hospital, it was nothing compared to the long-stemmed Calla Lilies in green and yellow he had all over her home. Her room had a new chaise lounge in white with green and yellow pillows. He knew that she loves pillows and had additional ones added to her bed. His attention to detail puzzled her and her friends. He seemed to remember everything she had ever said to him to the most exquisite detail.

She loved him more now than before. She stood there in astonishment with tears running down her cheeks, wondering whether she deserved all of this and hugged him to thank him. Everywhere was beautiful, he thought of everything; NXavier never left her bedside at the hospital, so when did he get to do all these things?

He had walked her to the shower and bathed her, washed her hair. Lorelei, a nurse herself, attended to her wound, and Mia blow-dried her hair and catch it up in a high ponytail since Orianthi foes not like to feel her hair touching her neck at home. He walked with her around the house a few times as ordered by the doctor, while the girls got their meals ready. They had lunch, and he took her to her room and assisted her down on her comfortable chaise lounge. Within seconds she was asleep. Afterward, NXavier went out to plan her week's schedule with Mia and Lorelei. He would do all breakfasts and dinners since he would be here with her at nights, and the girls would do her lunch and baths during their lunch breaks. He had requested the cleaning service to be in daily to do the cleaning and had commissioned the sitter to be here during the day with Orianthi for company. Mia and Lorelei were amazed at how attentive NXavier was to Orianthi and were happy she had found someone so caring.

Orianthi's girlfriends stayed over until after dinner but left as NXavier took her for a bath. She placed a cap over her hair and ask him to jump into the shower with her. She had enjoyed his baths, and she realized how much of an expert he had become in the past few days, but tonight, she missed feeling his body in the shower with her. She whispered that NXavier should get in with her, and he thought that she needs him to support her in there. NXavier quickly undressed and jumped in as she took the sponge and began to massage and lather his exhausted body all over. Then Orianthi peels down his foreskin and decreases the spray of the water to vibrate as she applied it enticingly to his hardened shaft.

He looked at her, pleading with her to hurry because he needed to control himself around her. It was only day 3 post-surgery, he correctly heard the doctor said no sex for 6 weeks. What was she doing to him?

Seeing her naked twice daily, bathing her and dressing her the past few days has driven him to the brink of insanity, he was unsure how much of her he can handle at this point. He took the sponge and began to bathe her to cool down his heated brain and lathered her body, and rinsed her skin thoroughly. After he was done, she rested her back into his powerful chest and lifted one leg onto the side of the shower to allow him access to clean her folds. She needed to feel his fingers inside of her dark crevice. The thought of NXavier touching her there made her body quiver in his strong arms held her securely. He ensures the water was at the perfect temperature as he applied the spray of hot water directly unto her hungry knob driving her insane. Then he spread her lips expertly with his fingers to clean between each fold superbly.

He sensed that she needed more, so he inserted a long, middle finger into her soft opening and enjoyed the tight, warmness awaiting him. NXavier wishes his erected member could feel this warmth since they had not made love in 11 days. He was praying for that invasion because his engorged member had navigated its way onto her back, opening between her wet cheeks in error. He wondered what she was thinking, feeling him touching her secret orifice. She said nothing but began to rotate her hips on his member.

He maneuvered his two fingers in and out of her until she was moaning loudly, pressing harder onto his stiff pole pressed against her posterior opening. He wished he could enter her, but this was not a topic yet discussed with her; however, his pulsating tip resting on her back entrance seems to arouse her immensely. She rubbed her body on him, pressing onto him, calling his name. NXavier felt his juices lubricating her back folds as she pressed into him. Apparently, their body was having the discussion without them. NXavier was as excited as Orianthi was to explore this adventure, but he would not dare do this to her so soon after surgery. He cradled her body supportively as she enjoyed her first orgasm after surgery.

He bent over and kiss her neck softly under the water, with a loud groan, she squirts her pent-up juices onto his fingers as he continued his dual minor invasions of her body.

The thought of their upcoming nightly adventures, along with her warm juices coating his fingers and the pressure of her body pressing onto the tip of his erected phallus, was too much for him. It was not long before she heard a deep growl escaped him, and he erupted between her cheeks, and he held her relaxed body under the soothing water. He turned her around to quickly assess if she was in any pain and realized a smile on her face as she lifted her face up to be kissed by her French Knight.

Chapter 12

FETISHES EXPLORED

Orianthi enjoyed falling asleep at night with her dark knight a few inches from her, their bodies entwined, she was just happy cuddling and waking up in his arms. NXavier only left her for work, errands and, I when he was speaking to the boys. NXavier had kept this aspect of his life away from her, and she respected his wishes. She still felt guilty for pulling him away from his boys on his last visit though unintentionally. She had the need to ensure that his children were not affected by her presence in his life. She loved him enough to understand if he needed to move back to Quebec to be closer to the children. She would miss him obviously, but at their young age, she felt they needed him more. She watched him reluctantly leave for work every morning but noticed how tense and exhausted he seemed this morning.

It was Saturday, 2 weeks after her surgery, and for some reason, he was working. She hated to know that he had to go in on the weekend. He worked the entire week, she was looking forward to having a relaxing weekend with him. Orianthi walked NXavier to the door and hugged him just a little bit longer that morning in gratitude for all he had done in the past two weeks. Her heart broke, knowing that he had worked on the dreaded weekend. She wanted to do something grand for him and wondered how she could repay him for all that he had done for her. He deserved to know that she loved him just as much as he loved her, and his efforts were appreciated. Lately, he had been wrestling with something, she had seen him lost in thoughts, but she just assumed his thoughts were about his sons and issues with his ex-wife; the only topic he clearly avoids discussing. The problems were noticeable, not work-related, because he talked about his job with her regularly.

After he left, she decided to prepare a romantic evening catering to him just like he had done for her since her surgery. Orianthi recruited the help of her friends to convert her home into an idyllic enclave for her sensual evening plans. Orianthi ordered more of her sensual candles, a selection of hot oils, rose petals, a silk robe, and new slippers for him. She hired two masseuses for a couple of massages to be given at the house before their romantic dinner. She drove to the adult store to retrieve a selection of assorted toys for the evening. She completed her purchases with matching robes, outfits for dinner, and the bed that was guaranteed to neutralize his stressful issues. She stopped along the way for an overdue manicure and pedicure and had her hair washed and styled.

When she returned, the house was spotless, exotic candles beautified* the entire home, the petals would be done before NXavier arrived. The two massage tables were set up in the sitting room, surrounded by fresh flowers and candles. The girls had all the ingredients waiting for Orianthi to cook. She prepared a meal of green fig salad, conch stuffed with mushrooms in a spicy vodka sauce, sundried tomatoes with bow tie pasta, and roasted vegetables with an avocado dressing. For dessert, she created caramel cheesecake to be served with a Guinness and Bailey's punch. An hour before he arrived home, she prepared the drinks, hoping that the Guinness would be an aphrodisiac. She showered and slipped into a silk robe, had his gown set out on the bed near his slippers. Lorelei did her makeup while Mia set the table and lit all the candles. Orianthi was pleased with their handiwork, her home was transformed into an exotic boudoir. The scent of Bath and Body Works cinnamon plugins permeated the air giving the house a Christmas feeling. She was ready to receive her King.

The girls slipped out just before NXavier's Mercedes pulled into the driveway, she hid the masseuse in the den and met him at the door with a drink in her hand dressed in a mid-thigh, red and black robe opened at the front revealing sexy red and black teddy.

NXavier stared at her in awe, took a long gulp of his drink, new drink, refreshing, and delicious, he thought as he licked his lips. He stared at Orianthi and pulled her roughly to him and kissed his seductive temptress deeply, and stepped onto the petalled sprinkled doorway. The entire house was lit by candles for as far as he could see from the front door.

He wondered what she had planned for the evening and was just grateful he was her man. He took in the spectacular view around him in amazement and prayed she did not exert herself too much. Here she was, only two and a half weeks since surgery, creating this romantic scene; Orianthi never ceased to amaze him.

Orianthi escorted him to her bedroom, where he showered and changed into his robe and slippers. As he showered, she alerted the masseuse to get ready and returned to escort him to their couples' massages. NXavier was quite intrigued by her thoughtfulness, yes he was tense and exhausted because he had been working ahead for his trip. He worked the weekend because he would be gone for two weeks and needed to clear his desk beforehand. He welcomed a massage because he had to leave for France on Wednesday with his family for two weeks and hated to live Orianthi behind. He has been aching to tell her but wanted her to be fully recovered first. He would hate to leave, and for her to suffer another setback, he would never forgive himself. He realized that he would have to tell her tonight, she seems to be in such great a mood, NXavier hated to change her mood, so he prayed she understands his rationale for his trip.

Once NXavier decided to tell Orianthi his secret, he relaxed and enjoyed the beautiful massage she ordered for them. NXavier could never get used to her, she is unpredictable, romantic, exciting, and refreshing. He hopes that the masseuse was not hurting her and asks if she was okay. She confirmed she was fine but left him to finished his massage while she disappeared into the house. After her massage, Orianthi set dinner on the candlelit table and slipped into her bedroom to change into the see-through number she picked up earlier today. Orianthi strategically arranged all the sex toys and gadgets on the bed and dresser for them to explore after dinner and lit the candles.

She waited until she heard the masseuse exited her home before stepping out of her room and walked towards NXavier, who was locking the front door. As NXavier saw the breathtaking vision in her sheer red nightgown and matching, lacey undergarments, he mentally calculated the weeks since her surgery. It has only been the second week, NXavier thought painfully, "how was he supposed to survive tonight with her dressed so provocatively?" NXavier was no longer relaxed, he was instantly erected, his voice caught in his throat, he felt flushed, he stammered as she handed him a fresh drink and guided him to the dining room. He could not bear to touch her; otherwise, the dinner would be forgotten, and he would be violating all her medical orders.

NXavier could not risk her getting sick, so he decided he needed a distraction, so as he helped her to her seat, he told her about his trip to France with his sons and ex-wife. NXavier incorporated how he wanted the boys to visit with his sick grandparents and how this was the only available time. He told her how it was planned before she fell ill, but he wanted to ensure that she was strong enough before he left her for such a length of time. She tried to scream, but she understood his reasoning. Orianthi felt like he selflessly maintains her needs, so she should comprehend his need to be with his family. She wants to make him as happy as he made her. Even if it meant him being in France without her, so be it. NXavier saw the conflicting emotions on her face and knew that she would never begrudge him time with his sons. He loved that affectionate quality about her, how he wished Orianthi was his wife, and that she was the one going away to France with him.

Orianthi wished that his co-parenting plans included her; she would have loved to visit France with him and his sons; however, his sons were clueless of her existence, and that was highly impossible. She would have given anything to be with him always but knew her paradise was him was only a Florida affair. He had a family that still included his ex-wife, parents, sons, and if she wanted to be with him, she should just be grateful for her present life with him. She feigned* some happiness for his sons and his parents, and turn their romantic evening back to them as soon as she could change the topic. She refused to sulk tonight, not after all the work she and her girls had put into this scintillating evening.

She cannot have Paris with him, but she will make the most of her days in Florida together until he leaves.

Dinner was as delicious as she hoped, and it was not long before his trip was forgotten. He loved her cooking; he loved her many exotic experiments. This Guinness and Bailey's drink did nothing to curb his appetite for this beauty sitting across the table from him, he thought. She was so understanding, and sexy, a powerful combination that made him wished that he could wipe the stuff off the table in one sweep, then spread her on the table for his enjoyment. He wanted her and needed to feel himself deep inside of her, a pity this could happen until the doctor released her. After dinner, Orianthi cleared the table and started the dishwasher, while he relaxed and stared at her every movement. He sat on the kitchen stool, wondering how he would survive his upcoming trip without her for 2 whole weeks. He has never been away from her for longer than 4 days since they met. The only time he is ever away from her was for work purposes or when he visited his sons. His heart broke every time he thought of living Orianthi behind. A feeling that was getting harder and harder to do. He is sometimes taken aback by his feelings for her.

Tonight floating around in the candle lights, she was more beautiful than he left her.

She danced around the house as she bent over to extinguished each candle. Even the way she blew out the candles turned him on. He was being tortured by the sight of her tonight. After she extinguished the last candle, she turned on the night lights and walked towards him. Orianthi fitted herself between his muscular thighs as he wrapped his arms around her affectionately caressing her naked back. NXavier rested his chin on her head as his fingers located the clips in her hair. He removed the pins and clips and saw her beautiful ombre curls of burgundy and black cascaded down her bareback. She realized it was time for her final surprise of the evening.

She refreshed his drink and escorted him to her bedroom. The vision that awaited him on the bed almost made him spurt his juices through his robe. Every inch of Orianthi's bed was covered with: silver balls, orgasm gels, pumps, whips, teasers, handcuffs, vibrators, rabbit ears, enhancement gels, delaying creams, strap-ons, butt plugs, ticklers, and pink ladies. He looked on the dresser and saw spankers, blindfolds, massaging oils, bath salts, oils and bubbles, lubricants, edible condoms, and underwear. NXavier smiled, pulled her to him to kiss her. He wondered where all these came from or did she have them hidden in the home before now. He selfishly hoped they were all new purchases because he would hate to think that she had previously explored this sexual aspect of her life with anyone else. The thought of Orianthi being touched by someone else filled him with dread.

NXavier look around him for a second and thought he had died and gone to heaven right in her bedroom. Yes, he has won the jackpot having Orianthi in love with him. He just told her that he was leaving for France on a trip without her, and she rewarded him with deepest fantasies. He was indeed in paradise. He tried to explore this aspect of his life once, but Jocelyne was not interested. He was petrified to discuss it with Orianthi for fear of rejection and the awkwardness that would follow. Now she had every toy he had seen in magazines or online in her room. Orianthi was pleased with NXavier interest in her expenditure. He sat on the bed and pull her down to sit next to him as they critically analyzed each product and decided which would be allowed, explored, or discarded.

For the next hour, they read, felt, touched, and explored the uses of each gadget. NXavier was so engrossed in toys he did not see Orianthi selecting their favorite items for an initial trial. She cleared out the stuff off the bed and returned with edible condoms and panties, a vibrating rabbit penile ring, and a pink lady for him. Then she chose stimulating oils, the rabbit ears and vibrator, and some beads for her pleasure. She escaped to her bathroom and returned with edible panties, nipples free bras, stockings garter belts. She stood in the doorway, suddenly shy as he looked at her. She knew that she was brave buying those toys but took on a huge gamble. What if he was not, and they did not share the same fantasies?

The animal look on his face confirmed his approval of her outfit, he got out of bed, removed his robe hurriedly, walked over to her, lifted her until her thighs were wrapped around his waist resting on his engorged phallus. He pinned her to the wall and lowered his lips on hers in a deep passionate kiss. Then he carried her to the bed and laid her down below him as they explored each other fetishes.

Chapter 13

AGONIZING DISTANCE

NXavier was living for Quebec on Wednesday to join his family for his trip to France. He knew that Orianthi was jealous of not accompanying him, but they refrained from bringing up the subject matter for the rest of their time together. Instead, they spent the remaining days discussing how difficult it would be to be away from each other for 2 long weeks. NXavier and Orianthi were inseparable on the days leading up to his departure for France. She dotted on him, and he spoilt her. He had never experienced this depth of love and intimacy before with Jocelyne and felt a bit guilty for thinking so. He enjoyed quiet relaxing days with Orianthi, she seemed to always have some new way of exciting him. They had enjoyed exploring their many toys in making alternative love to each other. He was amazed at the numerous climatic eruptions they accomplished without sex. They were still on the begrudging no sex for 6 weeks due to her medical rule, so going to France for two weeks will take away some of the pressure off him. It has been torture bathing with Orianthi, sleeping with her, making love to her without this final penetration. He hated being around her, aching for her, and not filling her up with his throbbing manhood.

By tomorrow evening, he will be in Quebec with his family, and he would have given anything in the world to see Paris through Orianthi's eyes. He hated leaving her for so long but was looking forward to spending time with his parents, grandparents, and sons. The only part of him that would be missing to make this a perfect trip was the absence of Orianthi. He could already sense the tension with his mom and Jocelyne, but he needed to ensure that everything ran smoothly because he was hoping to talk Jocelyne into leaving the boys with his parents until the end of summer; hopefully, she agrees. He was hoping he could convince her to visit her relatives for a vacation after he lives and let his parents spend some needed time with boys. The final night with Orianthi was a sad one. It was raining out, and she seems much more subdued than he had ever seen her. He offered to take her out, but she declined. She was not in the mood for any dinner, dancing, or games; she wanted to curl up into bed watching television. He tried to cheer her up with stories about his travels, which only seems to make her tearful.

She laid in bed, staring at the TV screen, but seeing nothing, she beckoned him to joined her in bed; he obliged and wrapped his arms around her. She turned on Netflix and settled for their favorite Gilmore Girls. She initiated no conversation, no explanation about the show, which was a norm for her. NXavier asked if she was comfortable, and she nodded her response but no words. He had never seen her like this, he missed his cheerful Orianthi. He turned her to him to kiss her and realized she was crying. He could not handle her being sad – jealous, yes, but her tears were unbearable. NXavier felt like someone had just soccer punched him in the chest, seeing her so sorry. He kissed her cheeks, then kissed her slowly at first, then hungrily as though the kisses would dispel* her distress. The sight of her tears evoked some deep-seated need for her, shamelessly, he wanted her more this minute than he had ever wanted her before.

He wanted to kiss away her anguish, kiss away her pain, kiss her until his beautiful vixen was back. He hated to know that he was the source of her tears. Orianthi laid comfortably in NXavier's arms, enjoying his delectable kisses, which left her breathless. Orianthi enjoyed his method of distraction, but she could not shake off this melancholy mood. Orianthi felt like she was losing a part of her, although NXavier was lying right next to her. She continued to cry not just for the length of his trip but because she would have no access to him in his uncharted life.

To be fair to NXavier, her tears were not entirely due to his trip, she was sad that he did not prepare her enough for his journey. She hated the silence surrounding his life, but she was watching the episode Gilmore Girls here Rory, and her mother had a huge fight and was simultaneously listening to a Macy Gray song in their rooms. Orianthi always cries when they are crying on that show. She did not feel like explaining this to NXavier, so she lay there crying silently instead. The crying was cathartic to her since she could not reveal to him the exact reasons for her tears.

NXavier rolled on his back and placed her on him. He wanted to feel her soft body on his. Orianthi rested her head on his bare chest, synchronizing her heartbeat to his, and inhaling his seductive scent. She laid on him for an eternity, then felt silly for spoiling their night. So she attempted to pull herself out of her depressed mood for his sake at least. He will be gone by the morning, she had enough time to be sad without him. Why start now? It was their last night together for a long time, she thought, let her make the most of it. Orianthi wanted NXavier to believe she will be okay without him. So she took the remote and switched to YouTube and selected Souskay's "Pare Pou Love," video then slipping off the bed, and pulling NXavier to dance with her. They both love dancing to this song. For the rest of the evening, they took turns selecting their favorite song to dance to. He is a fantastic dancer, and she loves dancing Zouks with him.

By the end of the night, they were showering together and pouring Bailey's all over each in bed. They were both sad by morning and spoke very little on the way to the airport. She walked him to the departure lounge because she could not say goodbye at the curb. By the time bid her farewell with a long, passionate kiss and hug, they were both in tears and grateful for the dark sunglasses covering their eyes. Orianthi watched NXavier disappear into the departure lounge at the Fort Lauderdale Airport, holding back the tears until he disappeared from her view. She had been holding back those tears since he said he was taking his family to France. She was not jealous of the fact that he was taking his family instead of her on a romantic trip. She was jealous because she had no access to this aspect of his life. Since his sons live with his ex-wife, she gets to go on the family trips, yes Orianthi understood that but the pain coursing through her did not get the memo.

Orianthi wondered why, after dating for so long, NXavier had yet to introduce her to his parents or any of his other family members. She listened to his answer about him not wanting his parents to dislike her like they did Jocelyne which was partly right, and she accepted his explanation, but some parts of her assumed that he was not ready to trust her in with details about his past, and that made her sad. She walked to her car with tears streaming down her cheeks unabashedly. She was oblivious to the world around her. Half of Orianthi's world was on a plane to Quebec, and the other half was in St Lucia. Orianthi had never felt as lonely as she thought now. She had three weeks left of her sick leave, Lianii was on vacation, her girlfriends were busy working. What would she do without NXavier? She could not imagine driving home and being there all alone. She would die of boredom without Lianii, NXavier, or work. The tears returned flowing down her cheeks, obscuring her view of traffic.

She saw the Davie exit and thought of Nova Southeastern University. She needed an outlet, anything to keep her sane for the next two weeks without NXavier. She didn't even realize she was driving, but she did and found herself in the parking lot of Nova Southeastern University. Since Orianthi needed something to keep her busy, maybe she should continue with her Doctor in Nursing Practice Education. She had registered in the program before but withdrew while going through her horrid divorce. She felt elated being back on campus, contemplating her future. She saw a few of her favorite instructors who were happy to see her again; it was not long before she was talking to a counselor, registering, and combing through the final year workload. She was less lonely now because she had so much work to catch up on to graduate next summer.

Orianthi knew that she did not discuss her plans with NXavier beforehand, not that he would mind since the school was a cause of tension in her previous relationship. Orianthi knew that NXavier would support her decision; however, she felt since he did not tell her about his trip beforehand, why should she be so open with him about everything?

She drove home to an empty house, wishing NXavier was coming over after work. Every inch of her home reminded her of him. His scent on her pillows, his robe, his towels, his slippers, his clothes in the closet. She decided to leave them unwashed for as long as possible so that she could feel a part of him there with her. She downloaded the necessary software she required for school, overnight ordered her textbooks from Amazon, downloaded, and reviewed previous course materials. Orianthi was so engrossed in her assignments that she missed lunch. She was startled by the sound of the telephone, picking it up she wondered why she did not silence the ringer.

Orianthi perked up when she realized it was NXavier on the line. He called to inform her that he had landed in Quebec and was heading home. She felt a ping of possessiveness when he said, "home." Orianthi thought his home was with her in Florida and hated that he refers to his house with the ex-wife as home. She quickly set her jealousy aside and listened to him fussing about her meals, rest, exercising, and relaxing.

Knowing that this would probably be the last time she heard his voice, she processed none of the details; instead, she chose to bask in his obvious affection for her. They spoke for the remainder of his trip until he said goodbye and left her again for the day. She could never get used to his absence; she could never be happy in any scenario which excluded him from her world. She felt guilty, not telling him about the school, but she was not ready for his disapproval because doing her school did not equate to the rest and relaxing as he advised. Schoolwork went against everything he told her to do. She needed a huge distraction from his absence of school was her best option.

□□□□□□□□□□□□□

NXavier walked in his home to boys squeals of excitement. They were so excited to be traveling later that he could not get a word in. The boys were packed and ready, although their flight we not for another three hours. He found Jocelyne in her bedroom, getting prepared and broached the subject of the boys staying longer than planned. She seems irritated about his idea but cheered up when he told her about visiting her family in Paris and living the boys with his parents. Their flight was uneventful, and he purposefully placed the children between him and Jocelyne so he could text Orianthi without her prying eyes. The boys were out like a light right after dinner, and Jocelyne was busy watching a movie on her tablet. He penned a detailed summary of his experience to Orianthi along with pictures that he had taken preflight. He bid Jocelyne goodnight and slept the rest of the way.

It was 4:00 am, and Orianthi was still up catching up with her assignments. She spoke to her friends in the evening the day before, about her decision to resume her education. As usual, they were in agreement and inquired if She required the company. She declined to have them over and went back to work. She heard her phone vibrate and smiled at the beautiful massages and pictures from NXavier. NXavier had sent pictures from both airports, pictures of his handsome sons, photos of an impeccably dressed Jocelyne, and photographs of himself. He sent some breathtaking views overlooking Paris, he took from the plane and those of the streets of Paris. She was ecstatic to see a glimpse of Paris. She will be less envious of his trip if he continues to share those images with her. Orianthi loved the pictures. She felt like she saw France vicariously through well-chosen photos. She stared at the various photographs and wished she was with him in the city of love. She drifted off to sleep, dreaming of seeing France one day with her beloved NXavier.

NXavier could hardly wait to be with his family, he missed them, and now that he was here, he was happy that Jocelyne recommended the trip. He needed to see them. A trip to his parents was long overdue, the boys are getting older and needed to spend more time with their grandparents and great grandparents before it was too late. His mother opened the door and burst into tears when she saw them. She misses her boys, yes they regularly FaceTime with each other it was not the same as to see and hug them in her arms. His mom was so happy to have the boys that her kisses in greeting to Jocelyne seem warmer. There is no love lost between his Mother and his wife, but at least they were making an effort. He took more pictures for Orianthi instead of a video because he didn't want it to send her any recording where she finds out the truth about his marital status. Orianthi finding out is his greatest nightmare. Everyone was quite excited to see them, and for the rest of the day, they caught up about news of their lives. ♡

His mom served a lavish dinner, which included other extended members of the family. The children were able to meet their other cousins around their age groups. The boys liked their cousins tremendously and were already asking whether they could have their cousin over for a sleepover. They disappeared into a room to set up their video games and left the adults alone in the parlor. NXavier looked around his family and saw how quiet Jocelyne was and asked if all was well with her? She nodded, but one could clearly see she was not interested in being here. He wondered why she had suggested the trip if she seems she did not want to be here. He excused himself from the table and rescued her from the table with a request for her to join him in their room to search for his medicine. She was relieved and quickly followed him into their bedroom.

Once away from earshot, she thanked him, bid her sons a good night, and headed to their assigned room. She changed into a seductive nightgown and asked NXavier to join her. At first, he thought she was having fun at his expense but was shocked to realize she was indeed serious. He stared at her blindly, wondering why the sudden interest in him? Did she change her mind about her feelings for him? He remained draped over the back of the sofa and asked her pointedly what her hidden agenda was? Was she in love with him again? Did she want more than the platonic co-parenting lifestyle shared currently? Jocelyne seems taken aback by his questions? She told him that she thought that he was overdue for sex and since they were in Paris, why not? Jocelyne did not say to him that she was just trying to confirm her 'Orianthi theory.

Jocelyne had not offered to have sex in over five years, they had not been intimate in three years, where he was questioning why she suddenly wanted to be with him. If it were anything like before, he would have been inside of her already. She was right! No, her feelings for him have not changed; she wanted to see his reaction to an offer of sex. She had no desire to sleep with NXavier. She was convinced more than ever that this "Orianthi" was real. She refused to answer his questions and turn her face away from him in the bed. NXavier analyzed the scenario before and walked out of the room, wondering if Jocelyne was toying with his emotions or up to something? NXavier spent the next two weeks observing Jocelyne, something was up with her. She was still distant with his family, indifferent to him, but at nights attempting to seduce him, which was so out of character for her. He suggested that she embarked on her vacation with her family earlier, but she refused, stating it would give his folks the wrong idea about their relationship. She was not projecting any useful reports being so distant here.

One morning his mom asked for a ride to the market, which signifies she wanted to talk to him in private. He always dreaded that "tête-a-tête" with his mother. She can see right through and decipher his and Jocelyne's relationship; however, he spent the entire time defending Jocelyne to his mom, knowing that his mom is accurate in her assessments. She began the minute they got in the car, asking him if he was happy? Yes, he was delighted with Orianthi, so he said yes. His mom asked him about Jocelyne's interaction with the family and whether he felt it was respectful? He hates questions like this because, as the mother of his children, he must protect her, but she was making it quite challenging for his folks to like her. His mother went into her usual rant about how wrong Jocelyne was for him and how she needed him to be happy, and maybe his happiness did not lie with his wife. She was in the middle of her ran when he thought he should shut her up permanently with his news.

He pulled the car in the parking lot, pulled out his phone and video called Orianthi.

She answered, looking so cute with her hair framing her heart-shaped face, her full lips, and beautiful skin. She was sitting up in bed on her laptop, surrounded by books. NXavier wished he was there to kiss her succulent lips. She smiled, and he melted, he was about to do something unorthodox and hoped she approved. NXavier enquired about her day then ask her to say hello to his mother. Both women stared at each other in shock for a second, before Orianthi said, "Bonjour Madame," Je M'appele Orianthi, Comment Allez Vous?" His mom answered her pleasantly in fluent English with a puzzled look on her face, wondering who she was. NXavier took the phone from his now dumbfounded mother and continued talking to the blushing Orianthi as if he was alone. NXavier enquired about all the papers around her, and she then confessed about returning to school. He scolded her for not relaxing as he suggested but was please she was engaged and contented.

He told her how much he misses and loves her how he had an enormous surprise for her on his return if she promised to rest. She begged for details, which he ignored and handed the phone to his mom to bid her goodbye. The second she was off the phone, his mom wanted to know everything about Orianthi. She saw the happiness on her son's face and in his voice and felt less angry. He swore her to secrecy then regaled her about his Orianthi. He informed his mom about the status of his relationship with Jocelyne. He told her about Jocelyne's comments about not being in love with him, which angered his mom all over again. He knew that his marriage was over, but the children deserved to be raised in an 'unbroken' home. He loved his boys too much to allow them to be affected by his decision. His mom agreed to his commitment to his sons, but advised him about being honest with Orianthi before she finds out, and he loses her forever. She secured Orianthi's number and promised to call her one day to see if her love for his son was genuine.

For the next week, his mother was more tolerant of Jocelyne's behavior and attitude. Her mother in law went out of her way to include her in discussions, asking for help with her cooking and made her feel as welcomed as one could for the sake of her boys. NXavier continued to be cautious around Jocelyne, never leaving his phone unlocked, always ensuring his laptop is shut down, and choosing to text Orianthi only when he was alone. It was a great relief on the entire house when Jocelyne left to spend the next month with her sister in the south of France. The boys were too happy spending time with cousins to miss their mother. NXavier spent an additional week sightseeing with his sons. He extended his trip, arranged to work from France, and took the boys to the Ethel Tower, Louvre museum, Cysteine Chapel, and every historical site he remembered before heading home to sweet Orianthi.

Chapter 14

SEDUCTIVE HOMECOMING

Orianthi did not complain when NXavier called about his flight extension. She was attempting to work ahead of time so she could spend more time with him upon his return. Orianthi paused for a second to ponder on his strange call with his mother. She was happy that he introduced her to his mom but wondered why the request was made inside of his car and instead of their home where she could meet his dad and grandparents as well. Baby steps, he is opening up about his family, let him do it at his own pace, she thought. For his last week in France, he called her every day, most times on video, because he wanted to see her, he claimed. He sent her videos of the boys, the sights he visited, and videos of family. Jocelyne appeared to be missing in all the videos, she noted. When she inquired about Jocelyne, he said that she went to the south of France on vacation with her sister while his boys stay on with his parents.

On the night before he left France, he was driving his mom home from an event when she requested that he called Orianthi. Orianthi saw his called and answered although he was clothed in a crop top and boy shorts, she had her phone on the stand while she applied lotion to her body. Xavier's mother was on the phone. She scrambled for a robe to cover her body before she addressed the lady. She turned to see both mother and son grinning at her, Orianthi blushed beet red at their obvious enjoyment. She greeted Mrs. Dimitri and pretended to roll her eyes at NXavier, which causes him to burst out laughing at her embarrassment.

She spoke to his mom at length, who wanted to know detailed information about her past, her present, and future goals. She answered all questions respectfully until she asked if Orianthi wanted children anymore. They had never discussed having children, and she paused and searched NXavier's face for a clue, but he seems to have drifted off into his own world, she said yes and saw him smiled. NXavier heard the question and silently prayed that she said yes because nothing would give him greater pleasure than a miniature replica of Orianthi. When she said yes, he wondered if he could ever love her more than he loved her now. She is back in school, he is unsure of how long, would she consider having a baby soon or after graduation. He brought up the subject matter later on in the evening and needed to know how much longer was school.

Orianthi admitted to working ahead of schedule, and the coursework remaining would be done at home independently. She had to attend a few mandated classes on Saturdays until November, but from November onwards, she would be working on her Thesis or Capstone project. She discussed her chosen idea of live streaming care to decrease the incidence of infection in the Thoracic Care Unit. He was intrigued by her passion for her work, and he completely supported her. Later on in the night, he called her again to help him along with a well-needed orgasm. He told her that by tomorrow night, he would be holding his busy vixen over his knee and teaching her the repercussions of disobeying his instructions. She giggled at the thought of him placing her over his knees and felt all wet just imaging NXavier being home, then thought of her potential spanking.

□□□□□□□□□□□

She hanged up the phone with Mia and sprung to action; it was almost time to pick NXavier from the airport. She rushed to the shower to get ready to pick him up from Miami International Airport and to usher him to his surprise evening. She silently smiled to herself, thinking of the night ahead. Flight of ideas rushing through her mind about being in his arms after three long weeks. Three weeks of no kisses, no touching, no hugs, no walking into his arms, and five long agonizing weeks of no sex. This was their period of pure hell. Orianthi had visited the doctor the day before, and he gave and all clear to resume sexual activities, so Orianthi wanted to treat NXavier to a romantic evening for his patience. She thought of all that she wanted to do with him tonight but settled for a cozy night at the newly constructed Hard Rock Cafe in Hollywood. They both were intrigued by the tall guitar building and promised to visit whenever the hype about the strangely shaped structure died down.

Orianthi called and secured a beautiful room on the top floor of the building, which boasts a hot tub in the center of the room. The bed was a huge California King size bed position right below an ample bay window, which provides a great view of the entire city. She looked at the pictures online and almost had an orgasm thinking of the two of them in there. A room on the top floor was pricey, but NXavier deserved it for taking care of her after surgery and for waiting for five weeks to ravish her. Orianthi had reviewed and approved the specific details she wanted for their night out with a hotel's personnel earlier. She chose to have the hot tub filled with honey- coconut bubbles with candles all around it on arrival. Have chilled champagne in a bucket along with two long-stemmed glasses, and scrumptious seafood dinner on heated plates for after their bath. She wanted the room dimly lit with petals all over the floor. She had selected the Pandora playlist of soft music she wanted to play in the background.

With just under an hour to meet him at the airport, she got dressed and wrapped her naked body in a coat, then grabbed a packed overnight bag for them and headed out of her home giddy with anticipation. The night air was cool to the face, no moon out, but millions of stars illuminated the night sky. She thought of him and wondered if she would ever get over how much he consumed her every waking thought. It was so lovely to have NXavier back. She had covered a considerable amount of her school work, so he was ready to relax. They were spending two beautiful nights at the hotel and heading out on Sunday. He was already waiting at the curb when she arrived. As she pulls up next to him at the curb, she felt all her nerve endings on edge at the sight of him. Her heart was racing, her skin was flushed, she could hardly wait to taste his lips. She held her breath for a second to control herself before getting out of the car to greet him.

When he saw her, his heart skipped a beat. Three weeks was much too long to be away from Orianthi, although she communicated with him frequently. He knew that he needed to stay away because he knew how torturous it would be around her and not ravish* Orianthi daily. He would need to use every ounce of will power he had to contain himself around her for the next week. She got out of the car to greet him with a red wrap-around jacket that reached just above her knee. The cleavage was deep, dress tied at the waist. He loves her outfit; she was stunning as usual. She had on a pair of sexy platform heels that made him insanely hard instantly. How is he expected to survive the week when she looks so hot picking him up from an airport?

NXavier looked down at her smiley face and pulled her to his hard chest and kissed her hungrily. Orianthi clung to him for support, she was stunned at how weak she felt in his arms. His musky scent filled her nostrils, her lips felt bruised from the bristles of his beard. He grew them the past three weeks, which makes him extremely distinguished; she felt moist in her lower region to look at him. He released her to get his bags to the trunk and returned to pull her to him again and kissed her. He kissed her longingly, forgetting that they were holding traffic until a blushing female police officer walked over to get them to move the vehicle. NXavier opened the door to usher Orianthi to her seat. He bent over to anchor her seat belt then stole another kiss as the officer shouted: "move your car!" NXavier made his way around the car, settled in as she drove off to the relief of other drivers and the impatient officer.

He reached for her hand and intertwine her fingers between his. He could barely keep his hands off her. She willed herself to drive because all she wanted to do was to pull off at the side of the road and let NXavier ravish her body. She was used to him forcing them, but she concentrated on the way instead. He entertained her with small talks about families and friends, but she found herself very distracted. She stole a few glances at him, and each time she felt a spasm rocking her inner core. When she took the route to the hotel, he questioned her rationale, and she told him that she was just picking her dinner order La Granja on the same street. When she pulled in front of the hotel, his interest peaked, and he looked at her puzzled. She beckoned a bellboy to assist with their luggage and got out of the car. He came out to look up at the magnificent structure, still wondering what she had planned. He was exhausted; he did not want a night out; he just wanted a quiet evening holding her in bed.

She saw the confusion on his face and ignored him. He will be just fine, she loves when he is unsure of her plans, he seems so pensive, yet cautious. He held her around the waist as they waited for the valet, and her body reacted to his hand on her skin treacherously. She handed the keys to the valet, checked in, and walked into the crowded elevator up to their room. They located their place, and he opened the door and walked into the candlelit room, soft reggae music playing in the background, rose petals scattered from the entrance to the California king bed in the corner of the room and tub completely surrounded with scented candles. A table was set for two, along with chilled champagne on ice on a nearby table. NXavier looked around the room in surprise and wondered if she was insane to bring him here on a night when she is still on restrictions, how is he supposed to control his libido in a room like this? The bellboy placed their bags in a corner then left.

She walked in and pulled him in with her, he was about to protest, she rested a finger on his lips and kissed him. NXavier wrapped his arms around her and kissed her forehead, hoping to curb his desires for her. She walked over to the table and asked if he was hungry, he said nothing. When she realized NXavier did not answer, she turned to enquire if he heard the question, but he was staring at her hungrily. She poured the champagne into the glasses and handed NXavier a drink, he took a long gulp and escaped into the shower, thinking a cold shower would subdue his needs for Orianthi. He returned ten minutes later, showered, hair damp, looking quite comfortable in a fluffy robe, looking hotter now than before he showered. Orianthi slipped out of her heels and poured him another drink then
walked over to him on legs of lead.

She felt like she survived the agonizing distance and needed to be with him, three weeks were long enough to be away from NXavier. She ached to be in his arms, being kissed by him. She could see the instant bulge in his robe and was happy that he wanted her as much as she did him. NXavier saw her walking to him, and his hunger for her returned with a vengeance. What was the point of the cold shower? She walked into his open arms, and NXavier cradled her body in his arms and squeezed her. He gently put her away from him to untie her dress then realized she had nothing on but red lingerie under her coat, no panties!

Her black nippleless teddy hugged her body and left nothing to the imagination. NXavier stared at her for a second before he lifted her and wrapped her legs around his waist, where she was intricately positioned directly above his bulge. He carried her to the bed and place her on the edge of the bed with her legs still wrapped around him. He lightly grazed his fingers on her wet heated snatch. He would love to enter her with one deep thrust that would match his need for her but restrained himself.

He lowered himself to licked and sucked hungrily on her moistened interior. Although his need was to impale her. He quickly undressed, and she flushed at the sight of his perfectly sculptured body. Her body shook with her need for him. She sat up for a second to put his massive member in her mouth for lubrication. They had the rest of the night to explore each other, and she just needed him to take her as roughly as he could.

Orianthi pulled him out of her mouth, then laid back and placed her legs on NXavier's shoulders, ready for him to fill her up with his pulsating rod. She stilled herself for the invasion, but he just stood there, rubbing the tip of his massive tool on her wet folds.

She writhed below him in anticipation, and he stayed at her entrance like he needed an invitation to go in. She angled him at her right entrance and arch her hip upwards, and saw the horror on his face as his tip entered her. He was shaking and looking down at her, almost frightened. She stopped to analyze his resistance and asked what was he waiting for, he then reminded her about her restrictions. In all her plans, she had forgotten to tell him she was cleared.

So she smiled and told him what the Doctor said. Orianthi could see the relief on his face. He was free to make love to her with no restrictions. He held her hips below him and lowered his pulsating phallus directly over Orianthi's wetness and entered her tightened hole with a deep thrust. She knew that it would be swift and hard, but she didn't mind, she craved for just that. They had two days to reconnect. He pulled out of her as she looked up to his face as he rested his knob at her moist entrance. She pushed off to meet him as he thrust his rod into her wet canal. She bit on her bottom lip to avoid a scream as he penetrated her slippery hole as she relaxed around him. She missed his thrust; she missed feeling him inside of her; she missed having him near her. Her body could not hold back as it betrayed her with huge orgasm the minute he filled her up with his hard tool the second time.

He never dreamed he would be inside of Her tonight. He thought he had to wait for a week. This was his sweetest surprise ever. He would be able to regulate his pace. He had no control tonight, five weeks was a long time to not fit into her, feeling her muscle tightening around his shaft. There was no substitute for her softness, nothing in this world compared or could compare to the ecstasy he felt covered in her warm juices. Her body got hotter and wetter with each thrust, and as she felt him tensed inside of her epicenter, her body rocked with her second well-needed orgasm. The spasms with her second orgasm were too much for him with a guttural groan he emptied his juices inside of her tight folds.

Chapter 15

REDEFINING LOVE

They spent two glorious days together at the Hard Rock Cafe, reintroducing their bodies to each other. He was a bit concerned about her when the night first started but relaxed when he confirmed that she was okay. This was their first sexual encounter since her surgery he would hate if she suffers a setback. He was gentle at first, but she urged him to relax. They spent two passionate days engrossed in each other, he seemed more open about his family then and called his mother in her presence and gave her the phone to say hello. He showed her all his beautiful images of France on his cellphone and reminded him of how much she wished that she had been there with him. He called his sons a few times to talk and listened patiently as they detailed their day with their cousins. This was the first time he ever called them in her presence. She loved this new NXavier who was a changed man, he was relaxed, open to her, she was beside herself with happiness. Once he was done with his call, she called Lianii and checked in with her friends for a few minutes as he ordered their meals.

He seems much more confident, comfortable, and happier now than he did before. The only times they were interrupted were the occasional visit by housekeeping and room service personnel who delivered their meals. NXavier was in heaven being in this exotic room with Orianthi, and being able to finally be with her in every sense of the word was exhilarating. He looked up from the bed at Orianthi, who stood at the window deep in thought, on Sunday morning, and wondered what was on her mind. She was lost in thought, staring at the view below; the view from the window was striking, the waterfalls, the pools, the designed below them were breathtaking. She was so happy to spend those sensual days with the man she loves. She was delighted to have him back and hoped that he was going nowhere in the foreseeable future. He got out of bed and stood behind her, then wrapped his arms around her. He looked in the magnificent view, and he was mesmerized by the view of the city from their vantage point and hated to know that they would be leaving it in a few hours. NXavier was happy at least to be back in Florida and have Orianthi in his precious arms, he thanked her for choosing the room, and for surprising him in such a way, he had a fantastic time with her, he always does.

While looking down at the city around them, he realized how happy he was with her, how much she meant to him, and suddenly remembered his Mom's advice at being honest with Orianthi. NXavier shuddered at the thought of being caught in a lie, which may cause him to lose Orianthi. Orianthi felt him shudder and looked up into his face and saw him frowning. She massaged his arm and rested her head on his shoulder as he lowered his lips to hers. She asked if all was well, and he reassured her that he was thinking about a work-related project. She patted his arms, which may have decreased his tension, and as they turned, they realized that their breakfast was recently delivered. As they sat for breakfast, he enquired about her classes, her capstone project, and her individual classes. She seemed so animated about her classes, and as much as he wanted to place her over his knee for not relaxing, he was happy she was content.

They checked out by 11:00 am, and he took her to his home for the rest of the day. He prepared their meal while she caught up on some work and his laundry, and packed some of his work clothes to take with her to her home later. They left his house after dinner and headed to her home for a much needed night's rest. They woke on Monday morning to heavy showers, so he opted to work from home. Once the weather cleared out, he received a telephone call and urgently left for his office. She stayed in bed on her laptop with her books around her doing some school work and was happy that it started to rain all over again. The weather made her wish he was home, she ordered her lunch, ate, and dozed off but was awakened by the phone. It was NXavier on the line asking her to retrieve some documents he needed that he left at her house. He wanted her to bring them to him at his office. She quickly showered and dressed casually in a beautiful sundress with a light sweater remembering his office was cold.

The rain was not as heavy as when she left home, and she thought that he would be waiting downstairs at the entrance for her, but he was nowhere in sight when she arrived. Orianthi parked her car in the visitor's parking and walked to the dreaded security area. Knowing how tedious it was to gain access to his office on the last occasion, though he was with her, imagine trying to navigate that route without him. When she got there, he was a meeting and had left instructions with the security to escort her to a waiting room near his office. She was alone in the waiting area, so she sat there texting her friends and enjoying the soft easy listening to Pandora music pipping into the room. Orianthi sat there impatiently, wishing that she had brought her laptop with her; at least she could have been working while she waited.

He swung around the corner 45 minutes later, extend his hand to her and kissed her lightly on both cheeks, and escorted her to his office. To her surprise, his photograph of his ex-wife and sons were replaced by a picture of him and his sons, and a photo of him and Orianthi in a passionate embrace. She stared at the picture of them on his desk and smiled at how important she was too him. NXavier was happy that he had replaced the photo of Jocelyne to a photo of him, and one of him and Orianthi, at least he got to make her smile. He loved to see her smile; however, her smiles were dangerous, and his heart skips a beat whenever he sees her smile. He took the package from her and motioned her to a nearby chair. He picked up the ringing phone and spoke to someone for 20 minutes while she explored the artwork around his office and then stared at the magnificent view from his window. She heard him put some ice in a glass as she walked back to his desk, and he handed her a drink, but he continued on the phone as she walked back to the window.

Orianthi heard NXavier discussing a trip on the phone; she, however, missed hearing the details about the location of the trip. When he asked if he could bring someone along with him on the trip, Orianthi thought he meant a work associate. Another trip, she silently fumed at the thought of being without him again. She tried to eavesdrop as much as possible for more details about his journey, but his responses were reticent to avoid giving out any more information. Orianthi did not think that she could handle another trip so soon after NXavier had only just arrived home from his three week trip in France. He seemed quite excited about the details of the trip as she silently stood fuming at the window staring at the rain in anger. How dare NXavier agrees to another trip so soon, she knew that he did not have a choice in the matter but was still angry. At least she has her schoolwork to keep her busy these days. Orianthi turned around to walk back to her chair just as he finished documenting the details and ending his call. He looked up at her face, and she could not even pretend to be happy for him, so she asked bluntly if he was going away and where?

NXavier sensed her unhappiness but was going to make her squirm before he tells her the good news. He walked out to his office clerk, collected an envelope from her and dismissed her for the day, walked back in his office and lock the door behind him, then beckoned at her to sit with him. She sat on him, trying to still maintain her unhappiness with his news, which was impossible to do being so close to him. He looked into her eyes and asked why she was sad, then brought her chin to his and kissed her repeatedly. He kissed her until the sparkle return to her radiant brown eyes, it hurts to see her sad, she mumbled between kisses some incoherent words about being miserable once he travels, but she knew that as a consultant with the firm he had no choice. He held her face between his two hands and asked her what if he could take her with him on his next trip, and what if the trip was to Martinique, how would she feel about his travels?

Her eyes lit up, as she shook her head in disbelief, he could not be serious, she had not been to Martinique in over 15 years and could not believe him until he handed her the itinerary, of a trip for two for 4 days, leaving in 2 days. Orianthi wrapped her arms around his neck and kissed him deeply, this was the most excellent news ever, they were going on their first trip together, and it was to her favorite place on earth, Martinique! She looked at the itinerary again; it showed the flight information, car service, and hotel. NXavier looked how happy the news of the trip made Orianthi, he never told her that the trip also includes a day in St Lucia, he will save that for later. She hugged and kissed him again. However, he was unsure of the catalyst, between the heavy showers of rain through his window or this excited Orianthi sitting on him kissing him, he became extremely engorged. He propped her on the edge of his desk, facing him and pulled off her jacket. Thankfully her sundress opened to the front, which provided easy access to her ample globes. He roughly slipped the spaghetti straps off her caramel shoulders, removed her bra to suck on her nipples.

He continued to suck her nipples and massage her jugs to the point of pain, then soothes her nipples with his warm lips and tongue. He cupped both breasts and took both nipples in his mouth. She was deep in thought and concentration as he grabbed a fist full of her skirt and yanked it up to reveal that she wasn't wearing any panties. With a pleasantly surprised look on his face, he grabbed her legs at the back of her knees and pulled her towards him. As he pushed her thighs wider, he realized that she was already moist from his nipple stimulation. He lowered his chair, drew her right at the edge of the desk, propped her back on her elbow, and placed her legs on his shoulders. She could not believe she was getting two surprises in one afternoon, here she was on the edge of the desk about to have him lick her, just as her fantasy.

Widing her legs, he leaned down and passionately kissed and licked her wet pussy. His lips on her drove her to the brink of insanity. While she succumbed to the pleasure of his lips on her, she felt his fingers on her inner thigh moving upwards. His fingers lightly grazed her outer lips. Then she felt him open her lips, feeling her moistened interior. Her clitoris pulsated, awaiting his light touch. His finger stroke and probe her stiffened clit. He placed a moistened finger at her entrance, and her entire body shook from the pleasure this evoked. She impatiently waited for him to insert his finger deep into her. As if he read her mind, his finger filled her wet hole, and his lips sucked her nipples. "She loves a finger in her" it felt so darn good. She was unsure which assault she preferred – his now 2 fingers thrusting into her or his lips on her nipples. She had no time to contemplate before her body shuttered from an orgasm. Then he slowly removed his lips and tongue from her throbbing hole and pulled her up close to him, engaging in a passionate kiss. His engorged member pressing into her.

She broke the kiss and dropped to her knees below his desk, and started fumbling with his zipper, thinking to herself what the hell are we doing, this is not the right place for this. But darn it felt great, she craved him so much, when he is gone, she tends to enjoy most of their time together. Though it was only 24 hours since their last encounter, she missed his touch, she wanted him so much. She would have been with him anywhere once he was willing. She searched for the source of the bulge that she'd been rubbing against. To her amazement, a large throbbing cock sprung into view. Without thinking, she grasped it with both hands, feeling the warmth of the throbbing rod in her hands. She looked up at him with a grin, and without a word, she dropped her lips down over the large head. A soft moan escaped him. She twirled her tongue around the head, then pulled the throbbing member from her full stretched mouth to look at it and thought to herself this thing is big! Then she started licking the entire length of it, after 3 to 5 long wet licks she took the head into her mouth in again.

Pushing herself a little further down the shaft. Orianthi felt it at the back of her throat with each thrust. He held her head tightly as his juices exploded out of his pulsating body down her throat and mouth. She quickly swallowed his essence as he brought her up to sit on his still engorged phallus and roughly filled her up with his enormous rod. She was wet and ready for this invasion. It was her Baby, after all, she loves the way he fills her. She loves him, fucking her. Within minutes he had her rocking with a second orgasm. He kissed her deeply through the orgasm, wanting to wrap her legs and arms around him, wanting more of her. She could feel every inch of his long shaft with every thrust. He turned her around and laid her across his desk and spread her cheeks and licked her holes hungrily. She enjoyed his expert tongue on her body, and she squirmed beneath him in pleasure. He doubled fingered her openings, which made her bite on her bottom lips to contain her screams. He withdrew his fingers, stood up, and impaled her waiting holes.

She stayed still and allowed his thrusts to continue for a minute then went along with the pace to hasten this assault. She could feel herself tightening with each thrust, and wanted it all to end. He shook her body with each powerful thrust as she clung to him. He positioned both hands under her butt cheeks to draw her closer and insert himself deeper into her. She felt the sensation rocking her core as she climbed to the edge as they both approached their peak. He could not take it anymore and thrusts himself deep into her. She yelled out in pure ecstasy as another orgasm consumed her. This also triggered his eruption, and he filled her up, holding tightly onto her as if his hips were glued to hers. NXavier and Orianthi kissed passionately, never wanting to let go. Maybe he will work from home more often if it comes with those midday treats, he thought, ad he held her limp body in his arm while their juices slipped down his deflated member.

Chapter 16

EXHILARATING SURPRISE

In two days, she will be in Martinique with her Prince Charming! Orianthi could not contain herself, NXavier was taking her along on first his business trip. Orianthi was running around, getting ready for their trip as if this was her honeymoon. She was grateful she had done the majority of her coursework for the semester to enjoy a weekend off. She carefully chose every outfit, shoes, jewelry for the occasion. She had the entire content of his suitcase cleaned and packed their bags by Tuesday. He collected the necessary documents he required for his meetings, picked up dinner, and headed home to Orianthi. They had a quiet dinner, a leisurely soak in the Jacuzzi, and an early night's rest. They were at the Miami International Airport at least two hours before their flight. They secured their seats on the airline, and she chose a movie to watch as he worked on his laptop.

The first-class flight to Martinique lasted less than 3 hours. After the movie was done, he shut off his laptop, and remove the armrest between them to allow her to rest on him. He held her snugly to him as she dozed off for the rest of the flight. They landed at 1:00 p.m., was received by a hotel employee, and shuttled to their hotel. This was a much newer and more developed Martinique than the one she recalled as a child. She could hardly wait to explore different parts of the island with NXavier. The hotel he chose was the exotic Bamboo Hotel in Les Trois-Ilets, a few miles from the city of Fort de France. The hotel was a majestic resort overlooking Fort de France. They checked in at the hotel and were escorted to their beautiful bungalow with white sand and the blue waters a few steps from their front door.

The bungalow was breathtaking, it was a quaint little cottage with a living room, bedroom, and bathroom. The room was equipped with a fully stocked refrigerator, comfortable sofas, televisions in both rooms, and an office area. The rooms had a rustic feeling to it, which made them feel at home. The lobby of the hotel was just a few feet away from their cottage. The hotel offered five different restaurants for their meals, but they had the option to stay in and order room service. NXavier arranged for a car service for his conference the following day, shoot some emails to inform the dignitaries* that he was on the island while Orianthi freshened up and changed. She chose an orange sundress which looked lovely on her. As she emerged from the room, he felt a stirring deep inside him. She was indeed a beautiful woman, but in Martinique, she seemed prettier. As she walked past him, his arms snaked out and brought her to his hard chest, she squealed in shock as he silenced her with a deep kiss. As their kiss deepened, she felt his bulge between them. She looked up and saw his agonizing need for her, she chuckled, and lead him right back to their bedroom. He undressed quickly as an impatient schoolboy. She slipped out of her dress, revealing matching undies, which made his engorged member throb even more. She rolled her eyes at him and joined him in the bed to quench his sudden burst of desire.

They emerged from their bungalow two hours later, content, refresh, and now starving. They walked over to the expansive* restaurant overlooking the water and secured a cozy table for a late lunch. Their meals were scrumptious, not that they remember to eat since they were lost in each other, deep in conversation, oblivious to time. After dinner, they opted for a leisurely stroll along the edge of the water then lay on two beach chairs to watch the sunset in the distance. The hotel boasted a famous night club which was packed to capacity when they finally went in after a late dinner, they danced to a few songs then retired to their bungalow for bed. Thursday and Friday were long workdays for NXavier. Orianthi used up her free time to shop, took a dip in the sea, visit the sauna, tour the city, and visited distant relatives.

At nights she would have dinner waiting when NXavier came in from his conferences. Having Orianthi waiting for him after a long day was the most relaxing moment of his life. Seeing her captivating smile always keeps him grounded. Orianthi would regale him with her activities of the day during dinner, and afterward, they would shower together and get into bed with their laptops. She would be occupied with school until he was done with his work, then they would turn to each other in a passionate embrace and make earth-shattering love to each other until they were both satiated*.

The Saturday, Orianthi woke up to the smell of coffee and bacon in bed. NXavier had been up early enough to go for a jog, and returned with breakfast while she slept. He was out of the shower in a robe, smiling down provocatively at her. She blushed, wondering how did she get so lucky to have such an amazing, intelligent, virile man so in love with her? He saw her blushing and tease her as he stood there, drying his curly black hair. He bent over to kiss her forehead and informed her that he had signed her up for a tour, which leaves in an hour to the volcano Montagne Pelee. He would not be attending because it was the final day of his conference. She understood but was disappointed. The last time she climbed to the top of the Volcano was at 14 years. She wanted to try again, but this time with NXavier.

She hurried breakfast and darted into the shower to get ready for the tour. He left for his conference before she was done dressing. She fished out a novel the minute the journey started and read all the way to Saint Pierre. They were now at the base of the volcano, she recalled lots of grass and trees here in her previous visit. The green grass and trees were replaced with a scenic route, gift shops, restaurants, theme parks, cultural displays, and sulfur baths, just like St Lucia's. Once they arrived and started on the tour of the site, Orianthi found herself lingering a little longer on the history of the town of St Pierre. She set off on the trail with the rest of the group. She was a bit distracted but can vaguely hear the tour guide's voice ahead. She wished NXavier was there with her, he would have appreciated the cultural history. The bus was set to depart at 3:00 p.m., so she thought that she would entertain herself and just meet with the group later.

She wondered about buying gifts for NXavier, Lianii, Zainii, and her friends. Although she had a hat on, she could feel the heat of the sun on her arms, face, and legs. She bought a refreshing drink, which did nothing to cool her down, she was feeling hot and sticky all over. Orianthi longed for a cool breeze, so she spied a lake in the distance and thought a quick dip in this beautiful lake nearby would suffice. She was not sure if a dip in the water was allowed, but the water was so inviting. She just could not resist a quick dip in its warm pool. She craved to feel the warm water on her hot skin. She was grateful that she had a bathing suit beneath her dress, and she had a towel in her bag. No one was around, so she quickly stripped to her swimsuit, glad to finally feel the cool breeze on her skin she slowly stepped into the warm water.

NXavier saw her wandered off away from the group and had been observing her and following her since she stopped for the gifts. He saw her stop for a drink and got one too, then followed her to the lake, who could blame her, it was smoldering hot. He watched her wiggle out of her shorts, and he got all heated up, staring at her roundly, shaped butt, and he longed to cup her cheeks. She unbuttoned her top and bent to pick up her shorts as he admired the way she filled up the bra. She bent over to place her discarded clothing on her backpack, and he felt a jolt of electricity shot through him. He imagined himself taking her in this exact position, but envisioned them getting arrested and stopped himself. She stood up and walked towards the water, unaware of his existence.

She stood with the water brushing at her nipples then closed her eyes to enjoy the serene silence. She was alone, the water was warm, clean, and quite relaxing. NXavier's conference ended favorably within an hour of him arriving there. He returned to the hotel and remembered that Orianthi was out on tour. He changed packed for the evening and asked the car service to take him to Orianthi. He arrived and went in search of her group but saw them moving on without Orianthi. She seemed to be so comfortable shopping and walking around all alone. He relaxed when he realized she was not in any danger; everyone appears to be relaxed too. He saw Orianthi turn towards the lake. The lake was a distance from the crowd and quite isolated, here she was bathing alone. What if he was not there and to protect her?

What if someone kidnapped had her? The thought of her being in danger chilled him. He had to remind himself that he was in Martinique, and not Florida, maybe she was safer here. He swiftly undressed and walked towards her, she seems so peaceful and relaxed he almost did not want to disturb her. As he stepped in the water, she was startled but quite relieved and elated to see it was him. She wondered how he made it here, and how did he find her here? She did not realize that she was asking these questions out loud until he began to answer her. NXavier walked over to his water nymph, stood behind her in the clear water, and wrapped his arms around her semi-clad body. She will ask more questions later, right now she was just happy to be in his arms, right here. She felt the fingers on her skin, fingers caressing her shoulders, and she inhaled sharply as NXavier brought his lips down to her neck. Her sadness at missing him earlier immediately dissipated with his first kiss on her neck. A smile spread across Orianthi's face when she realized how lucky she was to be all alone with him in this lake, in Martinique. She couldn't imagine a better feeling than to share this secluded lake with him.

He continued to trail light kisses on her shoulders and neck, and she craved to feel his lips on hers. She felt his strong arms around her massaging her wet skin and squeezing her globes. She loves being with him, she enjoys his fingers on her skin. She loves everything about him. He took them deeper into the water; now, the water was up to her shoulders. She turned around to face him and reached up to trace his lips. He opened his lips to suck on her finger. She was very grateful to have his arms around her because she felt weak as he started to suck on her finger. She closed her eyes, and a soft moan escaped her lips. She wanted him to kiss her, touch her, and take her all at once. He released her finger and bent towards her waiting lips. She pressed her body onto him for support. As he kissed her profoundly, she felt him releasing the clasps of her bra and freeing her heated breasts. His fingers knead on both squeezing each erected nipple. Her body ached for his every touch.

She longed to feel his lips on them, but this could only happen if she had her legs wrapped around his waist. She placed her arms around his neck and effortlessly cradle him with her thick thighs. She could feel his enormous shaft pressing into her panty covered pussy. He took both nipples into his mouth, and she felt the brink of an orgasm. She forced herself to wait for his shaft into her wet hole. She felt his fingers graze the edge of her panties; she closed her eyes and enjoyed his capable fingers pulling her panties to the side and felt the knob of his pulsating rod at her entrance. She steeled herself for the first thrust because she could never take him in with one push. She arched her back in anticipation.

She brought her lips to his, and as his tongue darted in her mouth in search of hers, she felt him fill her. Her body spasmed with her first orgasm. He held her through her orgasm but continued to thrust deeper into her softness. Orianthi held on to NXavier as he continued to pump himself into her mercilessly. She welcomed each thrust hungrily as if they were the only two people alive. Orianthi looked up at his face, and he smiled down at her as he lightly brushed the wet strand of hair from her flushed face. As he thrust into her, he knew that he could never have enough of her. She was very damp but extremely tight around him. He continued his thrust into her, he needed the sweet release that only she could give. He held her tightly to him, lifted her chin to kiss her deeply as he erupted into her. The force of his eruption sent her into her second orgasm.

Chapter 17

WILDEST DREAMS

They left the water, dried up, and caught up with the tour at the base of the volcano, then they proceeded to climb to the top of the mountain. The fresh air, the bath in the lake earlier, the heat, and his love being near him made the day perfect for NXavier. He liked to observe her in this environment, sweaty, relaxed, she was indeed an island girl, she appeared more alluring now than fully dressed for the evening. They climbed down the mountain much faster than they anticipated, and he had the car service waiting for them. They stopped at a nearby café for some lunch, did some sightseeing then the car drove them to the airport. Orianthi looked at NXavier in shock when he got out of the car and opened the door for her as he tipped the driver, who took two small suitcases out of the trunk and handed to them. NXavier asked the driver to pick them up at 4:00 pm the next day and escorted her to the counter to check-in for their surprised flight.

He avoided all eye contact with Orianthi and ignored her incessant questions by responding with "it's a surprise." It looks like he thought of everything, she thought, as he handed their tickets and passports at the departure lounge. She smiled as she saw the flight to St Lucia flashed on the screen at the departure lounge. A surprise flight to St Lucia, at least she would get to see Lianii and Zainii and her family. She could hardly wait to see the look on her parents' faces as she not discussed dating anyone in her previous calls. Her family is quite hospitable, so she was not worried about showing up with a friend. As Orianthi and NXavier waited to board the plane, he quickly filled the blanks for her on their impromptu trip. She wanted to know when did he set it up and how did he know what to pack for their overnight adventure. The flight to St Lucia was only 15 minutes, and NXavier had a car service waiting to take them to their destination. She was happy to be home at that time, the school was still out, the island was busy preparing for carnival celebration the following week, and the heat was palpable.

They were happy to be in the cool air in the car away from the smoldering heat. NXavier was in St Lucia with her, about to meet her family, see her childish home, she felt impatient and wanted the ordeal to be over. She got out of the car as it pulled into her parents' driveway, both girls were in the balcony, spotted them and run down the stairs to greet them. Their squeals must have alerted her parents, who appeared at the door to see the excitement and came down to meet their surprised guest and daughter. NXavier opened the trunk and to her surprise, retrieved the most amazing gifts for everyone from his suitcase. He instructed the driver to wait while they visited with her family. He loved to be in her home to catch a glimpse of her past and was enchanted by her lovely parents. He could see where Orianthi inherited her looks, attitude, and demeanor.

She excused herself to check in on the girls and their plans for the upcoming carnival festivities. They were excited, they told her they would be going in on Monday to watch the parade of the bands in the city with an older cousin. They were excited to see her but was but had prior plans for the evening. Since it was Saturday before Carnival, which in St Lucia was Calypso Finals Competition night, the girls had plans to have a sleepover at her aunt with their cousins to watch the show there. She hugged them and took some photos with them as evidence for Mia and Lorelei, who were unaware that she was in St Lucia. She swore the girls to secrecy since she was saving the details of her trip for a girls' night with her friends. She went to the restroom to freshen up, and when she returned, everyone was saying goodbye to NXavier and herself as he whisked a shocked Orianthi to the waiting cab.

Apparently, while she was in the restroom, he spoke to her dad about his surprise plans for the evening, who whispered something to her mom and the girls. So by the time she appeared it was a general consensus for them to leave. "What did he have up his sleeves?" She wondered. He promised them to visit tomorrow for lunch before their flight back to Martinique. As they settled in the car he handed the driver note and ignored her questions, and when she tried to use her charm for a response he kissed her to shut her up. The driver took them to the west of the island, and she wondered where were they spending the night? With so many hotels along the west coast, he could have selected any. She eventually settled down and gave him a tour of her island and enjoyed the ride with him.

The car swung into the courtyard of the Jade Mountain Resort, and she hugged and kissed NXavier deeply. She always wanted to visit this resort, the grandest on the island, it was also the most expensive. It was nestled below the pitons in the town of Soufriere, the hotel was as majestic as seen on previous. NXavier had heard the girls discussing a celebrity visit to the hotel while Orianthi was at the hospital. She was so animated talking about the resort that he thought surprising her for the night would make up for being away from her for a three weeks trip to France. NXavier tipped the driver handsomely and requested that he returned in the morning to drive them to the Sulphur Springs, to her parent's home, and then the airport before he escorted her into the lobby. They checked in quickly and were taken to the most beautiful suite she had ever seen. The spectacular view of the sea and the pitons in the distance was breathtaking. She could not believe they were here at Jade Mountain Resort!

Their room had a California king canopy bed with mosquito netting, and their wall facing the view was missing; there was also a small private blue pool a few steps from their bed. She quickly undressed and sank down into the warm waters before NXavier was done paying the bellboy for his services. He stripped, then took some photos of her and their room, and the view before getting them a drink and joining her in the pool. They stayed in the pool drinking and watching the incredible sunset from their room. They dressed up for dinner, did some dancing at the hotel then retired to their room where Orianthi spent the next hour expressing her sincere gratitude to NXavier for his surprises, and thoughtfulness. NXavier was grateful he visited St Lucia with Orianthi because the island was lush, green, authentic, and magical. They were able to witness the sunrise from their bed the next morning, and it was a place that he would like to visit again with Orianthi for more than one night.

The following morning, they set out early for the Sulphur Springs, the world's only walked-in volcano. Their cab driver was already waiting when they exited the hotel.

NXavier was mesmerized by the volcano and wished he could get closer as she explained the dangers of his need. They were joined by a few people and taken on a tour of the Sulphur Spring by a Tour Guide, though he hoped that they were alone. He enjoyed dipping into the Mineral Baths and painting their bodies with the Sulphur mud as they were told by the Tour Guide that it extracted impurities from their skin. He was extremely excited about sharing such an exotic experience with her. He could hardly wait to return. NXavier video called his mother to show her the splendor of the baths and described their medicinal properties that he read online while making their reservations. He handed the phone to Orianthi to speak to his mom for a few minutes before joining him in the heated mud. They checked off the hotel after 10:00 a.m., not before taking a short tour of the grounds and taking many photos of themselves in this beautiful resort.

They arrived at her parents for a lavish lunch of all her favorite meals, with her aunts, uncles, and cousins. Apparently, her mom in one day had arranged a feast and had the family in attendance. NXavier was meeting most of her immediate family in one sitting.

She was amazed at how natural he was in her natural element. After lunch, Orianthi spent some time with the girls leaving NXavier alone with her family. She returned to find him in a deep conversation with her dad. Her mom and aunts cornered her to asked about her night and her trip to Martinique and how she felt about her new beau. They gave their blessings and told her how comfortably he fitted in her absence. NXavier thanked everyone for welcoming him and promise to return soon for a more extended trip. They bid everyone a heartfelt farewell and headed to the airport.

They were back in their hotel room in Martinique by 3:30, and both needed a nap. It had been a very long, tiring day, and Orianthi was happy and grateful for his surprise. Orianthi did not realize how much she missed her parents and told NXavier about returning home for Christmas for at least a week but will be staying with her parents instead just to experience a real St Lucian Christmas. They slept until 5: 30 p.m. then decided to head to the beautiful beach since it was their last night in Martinique. Orianthi laid on the beach, staring at the crimson sunset over the city's skies, although she was blatantly distracted by NXavier's hard body swimming in the nearby waters. The beach was deserted this evening as the guests of the resort had left to get ready for the night's festivities. There was a concert later by some famous visiting artists. Orianthi loves sharing this beautiful private beach with just NXavier. She still could not believe he was in Martinique with her or was in St Lucia with her earlier. She could not ask for a better surprise.

NXavier's toned body glistening under the rays of light in the distance excited her, she was enthralled with how hard his body seemed with every stroke. The waters glided off his powerful physique in such a way that made her ache for kissing the water off his muscular-shoulders. Her body longed to be in the water with him, with her thighs wrapped around his lean waist. She just could not have enough of him. She could not resist, she was headed back to school and work on Tuesday, and was unsure of the state of her unit. Though she was out sick, she still occasionally worked from her home, creating the staff schedules and dealing with unit emergencies. She needed to be on the unit to ensure her unit was still intact. Orianthi turned her attention back to her panther-like, Adonis swimming in the water, how she craved to be near him, even with this short distance between them, her body still missed him considerably. She could not wait a second longer to be near him or feel his arms around her.

She stood up, removed her swimsuit, but left the wrap covering her hot, naked body. She secured their belongings and walked into the warm waters towards him.

She felt the heated water on her skin and felt flushed. Orianthi wished that this was their private beach, and NXavier could lick every drop of water off her chocolate skin. With the next seductive stroke, he suddenly realized she was nearby and extended his hand to her.

She walked into his arms, quite conscious of his firm lithe body, and rested her cheeks on his chest, hoping to stabilize her thunderous heartbeats. He lifted her chin and stared at her face, reading her need for him. He lowered his wet lips onto her neck and shoulders as he steadied her body from the waves. Orianthi loves being so close to him; although she is an island girl, she was not a fan of the sea. She would be petrified without his strong arms and chest providing a safe watery haven for her. Orianthi looked over his shoulders and could not miss the view of the illuminated city of Fort De France in the distance. She pointed it to NXavier and wondered if Quebec and Paris were as captivating.

Orianthi was happy to be sharing such a beautiful night with her baby. She held

NXavier and hugged him snugly. His skin felt like velvet on hers, she felt his lips lightly grazed her neck and chin, and she ached impatiently waiting for him to kiss her. She caressed his back and felt his bulge increase in size with each motion of the waves. She kissed his chest and shoulders and licked the salty water off him. He kissed her forehead, her neck, and she softly gasped when his lips finally met her hungry lips. With the first kiss she felt weak and breathless and clung to him for support as he deepened their kisses. She longed to feel him deep inside of her, to quenched the desires his kisses evoked. Orianthi wrapped her arms around his neck as he lifted her to shockingly massaged her naked body. He freed his throbbing member and lifted her weightless body to allow her to wrap her legs around his waist. She could feel his engorged phallus directly below her the tip of him touching her conveniently naked crutch.

His hands slipped to her hips and under her wrap. He caressed her button, and she lightly felt his finger flickering her clitoris. His middle finger impaled her epicenter while their kisses deepened. She lowered his summing trunks and held his hard cock. Every part of her body screamed to fill her up with his pulsating shaft, but she loves his fingers in her and didn't want to break the rhythm. She circled his dick with her fingers and pulled his foreskin up and down his taut member. With each thrust of his finger, she got closer to 'cumin' on his finger. He painfully removed his finger from her hungry hole for a second and roughly filled her with the length of him. She felt the pain of his intrusion split her. She stilled herself until she adjusted to the size of his hardness buried deep inside of her.

She rode his hard engorged member as much as the waves would allow. With every thrust, she got tighter, or he got bigger {blame the salt water}. His middle gently grazed her other opening, and she felt a jolt of electricity surged through her body. He held her cheeks open as he pounded into her, she craved to feel him feel her other crevice. He allowed the tip of his finger into her slowly. He was barely passed the first sphincter, and it was a mixture of pain mixed with intense pleasure. She was finally living a fantasy. To be impaled by her 'Baby' in every hole. She clung to his lips, her arms tightened around his neck, and she held her breath in anticipation of the final invasion. He lifted her off his dick and brought her down unto his piston at the same time filling her up with his finger. She felt hot, she was in pain, she loved the feeling of having him complete her. She held on to him, threw back her head, she was weak and powerless in his arms. She loves this man and loves how her body felt around him. She was in heaven!

It was too much for her; she felt her orgasm ripped through every fiber of her body, and her juices bathed his throbbing pole. She wanted to collapse in his arms and never leave this spot, but she had to will herself to continue to thank him for such pleasure. She formed a circle with her fingers around his dick, pull down his foreskin, and she increased her thrust up and down his firm shaft. His kisses deepened, his breathing quickened, she could feel him pulsating inside of her sore folds, and with a deep guttural grown, he exploded into her achy crevice. They just stood in the warm water entirely spent and let the waves roll around them for eternity. He cradled her body in his arm, brushed a strand of hair off her face. Orianthi looked up at him with a sheepish grin and wondered what she was planning as an encore since the night was young. He kissed her deeply before they walked over to their bungalow with arms around each other to get ready for concert and dancing.

Chapter 18

SHATTERED EXPECTATIONS

They left Martinique just a few hours after leaving the club at 5:00 a.m. on Monday morning. Orianthi could not remember the last time she danced this much. It was a momentous occasion because they were not blessed with one artist but a total of four for the concert. The artists who performed were Jade, VAYB, Phyllissa Ross, and Princess Lover, all her favorites. She was in heaven, as each artist sang her favorite songs throughout the night. Afterward, they danced in each other's arms long into the morning.

She was exhausted and could hardly wait to fall asleep on the flight home. They had a fantastic trip, and she was looking forward to regrouping with a night's rest before work the following day. They arrived in a very wet Florida, what a contrast from the past four hot days in Martinique. NXavier took her home, promising to get back later and left to check on his home and get ready for a meeting at 1:00 p.m.

He drove to his office and regale his associates about the benefits and pitfalls of an office in Martinique and left to shower change and return to spend the night with Orianthi.

NXavier arrived home to his television on and wondered whether he had left it on before he left for Martinique. There were also lots of dirty dishes in the sink. Surely he knew that he did not leave any dishes in the sink. Was there an intruder in his home? How long have they been there? He wondered.

NXavier was still trying to wonder how one of his fleece blankets made it to his couch when, to his dismay, his bedroom door opened and out walk Jocelyne. He would prefer the intruder. "Jocelyne was in Florida! When did she arrive? guessing by the pile-up of dishes, not today!" He thought. He stood there, staring at her frozen to the spot! What was she doing here? They stared at each other for eternity before she angrily demanded to know where he had been for the past few days and who was the woman with him? He stared at her wondering why was she in Florida instead of in the South of France with her sister? She hated being in Florida and had moved back to Quebec with his kids when he got this job and refused to visit him before now. Why was she here now?

He mumbled something about a business trip, but she was relentless. Jocelyne detailed how she had been in Florida for over a week now and has been following him around from his workplace to Orianthi's home. She told NXavier how she showed up at his job last Monday and saw him exiting with his arms around some woman. Jocelyne described how painful it was to follow him to another woman's house and how she waited for him to come home that night, and he never did! She remembered waiting for him on Tuesday and Wednesday then driving by to see his car at Orianthi's home. When she waited for him outside his office on Wednesday and never saw him, she called his office and was informed he was on a business trip. She then drove to Orianthi's home and rung the bell on three different days to prove she was not home as well. A woman at the house confirmed that she was with him on the trip.

By then, a tearful Jocelyne was screaming at him wanting to know how long this affair has been going on? NXavier tried to listen to Jocelyne, but all he could see was her obvious disappointment in him and an image of Orianthi opening the door to an angry Jocelyne. NXavier remembered his mother's words, to be honest with Orianthi, and NXavier wished he had discussed his marital status with her before now. He dreaded the thought of Jocelyne confronting her with the news. He absently heard Jocelyne comment about disappearing and taking his sons with her, which made his blood boil with anger. Taking his sons where?? He demanded she did not respond to his question. What does she mean by disappearing with his boys, he would have her for kidnapping in a second! He did not want to anger her any more than she seemed at this point, so he refrained from reminding Jocelyne that she was the one who changed the trajectory of their marriage for the past three years. She is the one who would disappear whenever he came home. She was also the one who was not into him and told him she did not love him anymore. Indirectly, she drove him into Orianthi's arms.

Knowing Jocelyne, he did not want her to carry her disappearing ♡ threat with his sons or confront Orianthi since she knew her home. He walked away from her and went

into the room he shared with Orianthi since Jocelyne seems to occupy his bedroom. She continued her screaming and fussing as he remained quiet throughout her outburst because he needed to think. How can he protect Orianthi from this mess that he has created and not lose her? He was grateful that Orianthi was back at work the following day, and there were fewer chances of being ambushed by Jocelyne at work. He was concerned that once he left for work, Jocelyne would make her way to Orianthi to inform her about their marriage, and he was not ready to face Orianthi with the truth. He texted Orianthi goodnight and dozed off and was awakened by a silhouette of Jocelyne framing the doorway in a seductive nightgown. He was shocked, wondering what her motive was.

He looked at her and wished that his body could respond to her. Maybe her constant rejections over the years may have impacted emotionally because, sadly, he felt nothing but respect for his wife. Why has she dressed like this anyway? He wondered. He was perplexed at her motive because for the past three years she had refused any sexual advances he made towards her. Was she suddenly into him tonight? He was very apprehensive about losing Orianthi to is loveless marriage but will not subject himself ♡ to appeasing Jocelyne's insecurities while she was trying to give him an ultimatum about his sons. He is refusing her tonight. NXavier got out of bed, apologies to his wife then stormed out of the room. He angrily walked into his bedroom and lock the door behind him. NXavier exited his bedroom in the morning fully dress and ready for work. NXavier wanted to spend as little time as possible with his angry wife. He greeted an even more furious, unpredictable Jocelyne who was definitely not happy about being rejected the previous night. She greeted him with her final demand that he terminated his affair with Orianthi this instance, or she would make their lives unbearable.

NXavier believed her because he had never seen this side of Jocelyne and needed to protect Orianthi from her. He also wanted to have full access to his sons. He hurriedly left in the middle of an argument with Jocelyne and was comforted with the fact that Orianthi was at work. When he arrived at work, he sent her a text and had his assistant arrange for delivery of flowers and lunch to be delivered to Orianthi on her first day back to work. He felt guilty at not saying goodnight to her or speaking to her in the morning, but his fear was worse than his guilt. NXavier called his mother to fill her up on his current state of affairs, and Jocelyne demands. His mother was furious that he had waited so long to talk to Orianthi about his marital status. The boys were still in Paris with her; she dreaded the fact that Jocelyne was using her grandsons as pons to make her son miserable. Mrs. Dimitri knew she did not like this girl for a reason, she hated the fact that she was right.

He was home on time not because he wanted to be under the same roof with Jocelyne, but NXavier wanted to ensure he contained her anger until he got a chance to speak to Orianthi alone. NXavier missed Orianthi, her smiles, holding her in his arms, kissing her, or just being in her calming presence to being here with Jocelyne. He knew that she must be wondering what was wrong with him, he saw her many messages from Orianthi asking if all was well with him. He tried to assure her that he was busy with work and had a lot to catch up on. Orianthi believed him because she was out for so long she did not recognize her unit. He sent her another text pretending to be exhausted and needed an early night. By the time Orianthi got home and called him, his cellphone was off. He fell into a pattern, short calls to Orianthi at work, when he was sure to miss her, ensured he texted or left her a voice note about working late, and phone was off at nights.

NXavier's schedule ran like this for the next two weeks. He pretended to be busy to avoid a discussion with Orianthi or a confrontation with Jocelyne. Jocelyne was happy to have him home with her every night, not that they spoke, but at least he was not running around with his playmate. NXavier was biding his time until Jocelyne left to go over and have a long talk with Orianthi and reveal everything to her. He continued to avoid her, and in the last week, he pretended to be out of the country on a business trip to Brazil to avoid her calls. NXavier hated lying to her, but what was the alternative? He was happy that she was swamped with work as well as and school to confirm his stories.

○●○●○●○●○●○●○●○●○●○●○●○●○●○●○●○●○●○

It was now three weeks after their trip back home from Martinique, three weeks since she last saw NXavier. Orianthi had his many voice messages, read his texts, received his flowers, and her meals, but could feel his absence in her life. She missed being near him, being in his arms, his lips on hers, or falling asleep in his arms. Regardless of how late he stayed at his office in the past, he would always call her before bed. Now not only was he not calling, but he was also shutting off his phone at nights, which was new for him. She wondered whether he was dealing with something at work? Was the issue with his family? Orianthi knew that something was wrong; it was unlike NXavier to stay away from her for so long. She talked about his behavior with her girlfriends, and the general consensus was something was up. Something was definitely up. She spent hours wondering about him but knew that he would confide in her when he was ready. Orianthi was busy with work, which provided a great distraction to missing NXavier as she did. She allowed this schedule to continue for another two weeks; however, she wanted to know if all was well. She threw herself into work and school to distract herself and prepared for Lianii to return for school in a few days. During the weekdays she worked at stabilizing her unit and completing her coursework, and on weekends she spent time with Lorelei or Mia.

To be honest, she spent more time staring at her phone every second for a message or a call from NXavier, but none came. Jocelyne remained with him until it was time to head back to France to take their sons home. She had ironed out their differences, but her ultimatum remained. Either he stayed away from Orianthi, or he would live to regret it. He was waiting for Jocelyne to leave for France on Sunday to have a long talk with Orianthi. He believed Jocelyne's threats, and as much as he hated giving in to Jocelyne's demands, he could not expose Orianthi to them, not if he could help it. NXavier would give Orianthi all the facts when he saw her next and hoped for the best outcome. One thing he knew, he dreaded this upcoming conversation with Orianthi. The thought of losing her was paralyzing. He needed her for survival, although he had been home with Jocelyne for three weeks, now he is convinced without the boys they have nothing in common. He missed Orianthi!

On Saturday afternoon, a day before Jocelyne's departure, she was in the kitchen preparing dinner for them while NXavier was working in his study. NXavier was speaking on FaceTime to his sons and parents when they heard a knock on the front door.

Orianthi needed to deal with his absence or confront NXavier, whichever one comes first. It was three weeks now for crying out loud. She needed some answers because his absence was crippling her. Before then, she was in bed with her books, but everything and everywhere reminded her of him. She called his phone, no response, she called at work and was told he was at home, so she decided to drive over to his house.

On the ride over, she wondered if he was sick, nothing prepared her for his actual reason. She parked behind his car in the driveway and rang the doorbell waiting for NXavier to answer, but the door was opened to her surprised by a very comfortable Jocelyne who apparently knew of her. At first, she thought Jocelyne bought his sons with her until she heard NXavier's voice talking to his mom and son. Jocelyne was there without boys! She was about to ask for NXavier when Jocelyne rudely asked, "What are you doing here? What do you want with my husband?"

Orianthi stood there in shock, she observed the current scene as if she was in a dream. NXavier is married? This could not be happening; why didn't he tell her? Then she heard Jocelyne say "Stay away from her husband your homewrecker!" as she felt the blood drained from her face. She could not get past the "HE IS MARRIED" bit. They were married to each other. The trips, the no calls from Quebec, the journey to France with her, it was because they were married. NXavier has been lying to her? She felt weak and nauseous from the revelation of knowing she was just a side fling, his mistress, nothing more. She thought Jocelyne was in France. How long has she been here? Who cares where Jocelyne was, NXavier is married! Orianthi felt faintish, how could she have let this happen? NXavier was in his study when he heard Jocelyne voice, he wondered who was at the door, he never thought it would be Orianthi. He heard her say, husband, so he walked to the door and saw Orianthi standing there with her eyes closed white as a sheet. Orianthi felt the tears sting the back of her eyelids as she listened to Jocelyne's hurtful words.

She wanted to run to her car but could not move, she was paralyzed. Orianthi did not even realize her eyes were shut. She needed to contain herself because she did not want to cry now, she would on her drive home. She kept on hearing Jocelyne's words, and she could only shut them off by shutting her eyes. When she opened them NXavier was standing behind Jocelyne, staring at her blankly. The neighbors were staring at her embarrassed for her. One look at NXavier's shocked face confirmed Jocelyne's comments. She turned away from his doorway and headed to her car as Jocelyne bang the door in her face. The expression on NXavier face seems to have given her the strength to move. She could hear Jocelyne's voice screaming about the nerve of her to visit their home and asking NXavier whether Orianthi had been in here before.

Orianthi made it to her car and burst into tears, all she could think of was her NXavier was still married and never told her. It had all been lies, the love, their laughs, her happiness. How gullible was she to believe when he let her speak to his mother, he was single? It all made sense, his reluctance to discuss his life with her, his lack of calls on his many trips to Quebec, and France. He was playing her all along. Why allow her to fall in love with him when he knew he was not free to give himself entirely to her. Orianthi thought that she had met her prince charming only to realize now their relationship was just a huge lie.

Through her tears, she called Mia and Lorelei to see who was free and at home.

She found Mia and tearfully fill her up on the events of her visit to NXavier's home as she drove. Orianthi could not bear to be at her home, too many memories there, so she stopped to get some clothes and her laptop to stay with Mia for the next few days. She does not recall driving or stopping for her belongings, the tears streaming down her face, blinding her at times. Mia kept her talking until she got to her home. NXavier called a few times, but she was not in the mood to hear more lies at this point, so she blocked him. He called Mia, who blocked him as well. Orianthi felt broken, alone, and flooded as she pulled in Mia's driveway.

Chapter 19

AGONIZING AFTERMATH

Mia met a broken Orianthi downstairs and wrapped her arms around her. She could not recall ever seeing Orianthi so frail in the decades that she knew her. Her heart ached for her tearful friend. Mia escorted Orianthi to her guess bedroom and tucked her in bed, then placed her laptop and charged her phone within reach, knowing that Orianthi may work through her sorrows. Orianthi had spent many nights with her before today, and this was the first time Orianthi was in no mood to talk to her. Mia walked out of the room and returned with two glasses of red wine to drown their pain. She had been best friends with Orianthi since high school, and not once through their many heartbreaks had she ever seen Orianthi so unhappy.

She knew how much Orianthi loved NXavier and trusted him, he had been dating her for a year, and they all loved the way he treated Orianthi. Mia called Lorelei to keep her abreast with present status and then held her weeping friend until she drifted off to sleep.

After work, Lorelei stopped to park an overnight bag and headed to Mia's house to help console her friend. She ordered Sushi for their dinner as she knew Orianthi loved Dragon Rolls with the hope that the sushi would cheer her up a bit since, according to Mia, it would be a very long night.

Thankfully, Lorelei's husband was out of town on a business trip, and Zainii was still in St Lucia, which meant she was free to head over to Mia's to help comfort her friend. When she arrived, Mia was quietly observing Orianthi while she restlessly tossed and turn in her sleep. Orianthi seemed to be tortured even in her sleep, and it was sad to see the occasional tears roll down her stained, chubby cheeks while sleeping. They walked away, wondering how they would pull their friend over this terrible huddle.

Orianthi slept until 11:00 p.m., and she turned on the night lamp wandered aimlessly around the room. She missed her room, she missed her bed, and most of all, she missed NXavier. The tears flowed down her face at the mere thought of him. She had a throbbing headache to accompany the pain in her heart. She felt like her entire world was shattered and torn to shreds. Like someone had taken a long double edge sword and drove it deep into her heart. She stripped and stepped into the shower for a hot bath. Just maybe the bath would erase the events of the day – NXavier is Married! She kept on having flashbacks of Jocelyne's words over and over in her mind, and they hurt every time she hears them. She could not forget the image of NXavier distraught face, staring at her, not denying the hurtful words echoed from Jocelyne. He looked like a shell of himself just standing there while Orianthi felt like someone was pushing their hand into her chest and reaping out her heart.

The pain was so real that the only remedy for her was a continuous glass of red wine and sleep. Even in sleep, she kept on re-experiencing the earlier scenario. She was standing under the water for a long time, allowing the pain to dissipate from her body when she realized that both of her friends were in the bathroom observing her. They had heard her in the shower and entered the bathroom to curiously check on her. She is so grateful for them and doesn't know what she would have done without them as needed to rely on them for strength to get through this rug being pulled underneath her. Orianthi sensed her friends without turning around; she knew they were concerned about her; as expected, she was just not ready to talk about it as yet.

Orianthi came out eventually and asked her friends why they were still awake? She knew the answer before asking as none of them could sleep if one of them were hurting. They had never seen Orianthi so quiet, and they were now worried about her. She had not eaten since she came over except for the wine that she drank earlier. Her friends felt so helpless, waiting for Orianthi to talk, but she said nothing. Orianthi wished that this was all a dream, she hoped that NXavier could walk through the door at any second and wipe away all the pain that she felt, however, he could not, he was married, NXavier had a wife, he was married to the mother of his sons, same woman who thinks of her as a homewrecker. He never told her he was married; how could she be a homewrecker when he told her was divorced! NXavier is online profile said he was divorced! He created this nightmarish hell and was nowhere to fix it. She would not even consider dating a guy who is separated, much less to date and fall in love so hopelessly with a married one is unheard of in her book. She feels so stupid at this point, she let him meet her friends, her daughter, her coworkers knew him, worse of all he met her parents!

Orianthi recalled NXavier telling her that he had not had sex in two years when they first met. Was this a lie too? She wondered. So many things were going through her head, she should have felt better after the nap, but it felt like she was still at his house listening to his wife; like time stood still while her tears flowed to accompany the pain. They had never even had a fight, and she was so happy with him. Did she miss some signs about him? How did she miss he was married? How gullible he must have thought of her. She asked her friends if NXavier had called them and smiled, learning her friends had also blocked him. They refrained from telling her that NXavier had been over twice and was turned away on both occasions by her friends. He brought huge bouquets of flowers, many gifts, letters, cards, cheesecake, desserts, her favorite wine, chocolates, and chocolate-covered strawberries to see her explain. He had thought of it all.

NXavier made numerous attempts to see Orianthi throughout the day, and with each visit, he was told that Orianthi was distraught but asleep, and he would not be allowed to see Orianthi, in spite of his persistence. Her friends chose to accept the numerous gifts and flowers he brought with each visit because he appeared to be remorseful and hoped that Orianthi would forgive them for taking the gifts. They placed all his trinkets in the living room for Orianthi to deal with when she was ready. It was painful watching how sad he appeared, but he lied to their friend and destroyed her, so right now, their loyalty was to her. They thought to inform her of the NXavier's many visits in the morning when her avalanche of tears stopped. They could not let NXavier see her, not while she was so distraught about his lies. He hurt her, he does not get to see her feel better about himself. They wanted him to suffer as much as she was right now. They had to protect their girl, she was hurting now, and they would do anything to take her pain away.

Orianthi felt a flicker of happiness, learning that her friends had blocked NXavier as well. She could always count on those two to have each other's back regardless of the circumstance. Orianthi was not in any frame of mind to hear his voice as she was too vulnerable at this time. Orianthi felt that she would unblock him only when she is ready to thoroughly entertain his rationale. She was head over heels in love with NXavier, so in all actuality, distancing herself was her only protection. She could not think straight with him within a mile of her. She walked into the kitchen and stared out of the window at the city lights with her friends trailing behind her. She wondered if someone else with similar pain was staring out at the lights like she was.

It was raining heavily out, which totally mirrored her tears. It is so uncanny how it always rained when she is sad or in pain. Tonight the rain reminded her of the night of her surgery when she did not know the whereabouts of NXavier. She missed NXavier as much as she was hurting. How could he have loved her the way he did and lie to her? Why didn't he feel comfortable enough to confide in her? She had so many unanswered questions, she definitely needed more wine. She walked to the refrigerator and was shocked to find all her favorite, cheesecake, sushi, dragon rolls, and bottles upon bottles of Maneschewitz, her favorite red wine. Her friends truly knew her choice, and they were going out of their way to cheer her up. She was right to come over, knowing that NXavier would be over to her house the second he could escape to try and lie to her some more.

She was not interested in being lied to again by NXavier or anyone else tonight.

She grabbed a bottle of red wine and walked back to the room with two glasses. Mia and Lorelei followed her and sat at the edge of the bed hoping she was willing to talk. The sounds of the thunder outside seem to calm her aching heart. She stared at the window waiting for the next lightning and sipping on her wine. She wished that she was at home alone – alone to enjoy the rain, alone with her thoughts, alone to daydream about the good old days.

She was lost in thoughts when she heard Mia's voice. The sounds of her voice brought her crushingly back to reality. The tears forcefully flowed down her cheeks, and she cuddled on her body pillow. Orianthi continued to cry as Mia's voice trailed off, she never responded to her friends. Eventually, they hugged her and walked out of the room, leaving her in her melancholic state, rain, thunders, and lightning.

When she woke up, she turned on the television directly to Netflix and clicked onto Gilmore Girls. She was sure that it would not be long before the girls on the show would be in tears. She needed the Gilmore Girls tonight. It was not long before she escaped into one of their scenarios and felt transported to Star's Hollow, Connecticut, just like everyone else on the show. She drifted off and work up to a rainy morning, it was also dark out, but with the new day came new awareness. She was single and had been living a lie. She was tearless for the first time since the rude awakening the day before. She was also hungry since she ate nothing the day before which gave her a pulsating headache from her excessive drinking the previous night.

She freshened up and left to make herself a huge cup of coffee. As Orianthi walked to the kitchen, she was startled by an incessant knock at the door. She looked around the house, and the girls were still asleep, so she went over and opened the door. Standing, there was a wet NXavier with Starbucks coffee and bags of stuff. They stared at each other in muted surprise, both too paralyzed to speak. He was not expecting her to open the door and she was not expecting him to be there. She eventually found her strength and slammed the door in his face without uttering a word, and turn around angrily to see Mia and Lorelei standing a few feet from her. How dare he show up with coffee, even in pain, her treacherous, broken heart wished to pull him out of the rain, dry him up, and hug him. No! She just couldn't, he deserved to be outside in the rain. She was not ready to see him, she was not strong enough for any confrontation with him, not when her treacherous heart still wants to dry and hug him.

She walked to her room and locked her door until she heard his car drove in the distance. She muted the television and waited until her friends were free to explain to her why NXavier was at the door carrying three cups of coffees and bags of her favorite pastries. As she stormed out to face her friends, they were busy displaying the beautiful pastries and beverages that NXavier brought over. The aroma was intoxicating. Yes, she wanted to hate him, but her mouth and stomach were doing somersaults in anticipation of the tasty meal. She refused to eat until the girls gave her an explanation to why NXavier was there in her hidden world away from him? She was still complaining about how ridiculous it was for him to think he could just bring coffee, and she would welcome him as if the activities of the previous day were insignificant when Mia stood up and without a word dragged Orianthi to the rest of her home.

Every living space in Mia's house was covered with flowers, gift bags, fruit baskets, boxes, cards, and letters. She stood there flustered, wondering when did all those arrive without her knowledge. With tearful eyes, she turned to Mia who wrapped her arms around her saddened and conflicted friend. They walked back to the kitchen for breakfast as her friends updated her on NXavier activities of the previous day. She was not amused at his assumptions that his gifts, flowers, and other trinkets could have erased his betrayal.

Since he had infiltrated her sanctuary by coming over, Orianthi decided to get the girls to help her transport all her gifts and flowers to her home. She figured if NXavier could come to Mia's, she may as well go to her house, her bed, her tub. She opened her door to a similar vision in her home. Gifts and fruit baskets everywhere. She asked Mia and Lorelei to keep some of the fruits to take home with them as they unpacked the remaining stuff from their cars.

The girls longed to see what NXavier had in the many gift bags, but Orianthi chose not give NXavier the satisfaction of opening his gifts that day or ever. She was in no mood to get a glimpse of a world that was never hers. His many gifts had only proven how guilty he was, and how happy he could make her as a dutiful mistress, and she was the homewrecker that his wife described. He should have given her the option to be his mistress, her discussion, she hated being left in the dark. She needed to forget NXavier for now, for the day. She intended to take a long hot bath to relax her body and soothe her aching soul. After her bath, she would jump into her bed and resume watching her Gilmore Girls. As Orianthi walked towards her room, she instructed her girlfriends to open and catalog of all the gifts NXavier left and place them in the spare room. She thanked her friends for their help as she disappeared in her bedroom for a deep soak in her heated tub.

Chapter 20

ILLUSIVE DISTANCE

NXavier watched Jocelyne get into a cab on a Sunday morning and was relieved to see her leave. He was up to his head with her threats of disappearing with his sons. NXavier did not want her to use their children as a pawn, did not want their lives to change, and was worried about Jocelyne poisoning their immature minds about him as he loved his sons immensely. He wished that he could divorce Jocelyne and get the visitation of his sons, but then they would be with him only part-time, which may impact them academically. It would break his heart if his sons were affected by his actions. He also loves Orianthi, who now wants nothing to do with him and who blocked him and just banged the door in his face that morning. He was so happy to see her standing at the door, but he could not say anything to her, he could not, it was too soon and he didn't know what to say.

Jocelyne demanded that NXavier leave his job in Florida and move back to Quebec with her and the kids if he wanted to continue seeing them. The last thing Jocelyne wanted was for him to be in Florida running around with Orianthi. NXavier had previously thought of the likelihood of quitting his job and moving back to Quebec with no chance of seeing Orianthi; however, that was too torturous to think of, so he adamantly said no. Jocelyne was not one to be outdone under any circumstance, suggested that if he would not move back to Quebec to be a family and care for his sons, no longer would she sacrifice her life raising their children alone while he ran around with some other trump. Jocelyne practically informed him that she would be moving back to Florida with their sons by the end of the term. NXavier could not refuse her this option because the final choice was the divorce that he dreaded.

When Orianthi left his house in tears the day before, he felt so helpless, so trapped and frozen. For a few minutes afterward, he could not move; the entire scenario seemed surreal to him.

Why was Orianthi here?

She had never visited his home without him before.

Why didn't she call him first?

He was not prepared for his relationship to be exposed to Jocelyne until after he was divorced from her. He knows that he loves her and wanted to spend the rest of his life with Orianthi but would wait for his sons to get older when they could truly understand his decision. Instead, he stood there and watched everything he had worked so hard to cultivate with Orianthi destroyed in one minute. He called his mother, who scolded him about not being honest with Orianthi, as she requested weeks ago. She was furious at Jocelyne's comments about disappearing with her grandbabies.

NXavier hanged up the phone wishing that he could call Orianthi; he missed holding her, kissing her, lying in bed next to her. Orianthi had filled such a huge part of his life lately that he does not know how he would refill the void her absence has left. He had tried on many occasions to see her or apologize to her, but she refused to see him. He was so distracted that his work was suffering. He needed to see her soon because not talking to her or seeing her was suffocating. How could she live without hearing his voice, talking to him, and seeing him? In all honesty, he existed only as a shell of his previous self without her! NXavier was contemplating visiting Orianthi at her hospital; this seemed to be his only option. He may have to show up at her workplace and force a conversation with her there.

. . . .

Orianthi decided to ignore all contact with NXavier for the next few weeks. She continued to block all his access to her phone and social media.

She refused to read his many cards delivered at her door and refuse to open his gifts. Every one of his trinkets was placed in her guest room with the original gifts unopened. She changed the locks on her doors because he had keys to her home and blatantly refuse to open her doors to his futile knockings. He met her at her doorway one night after work, and she walked through her door and left him standing outside. She knew that he deserved to get a chance to explain his lies and betrayal of her trust, but why should he feel better when she was still broken?

Orianthi could not forget his lack of defenses at her attack by Jocelyne.

She kept replaying Jocelyne's words in her head over and over again and kept on seeing NXavier's face just standing there, failing to defend her from the assault. He lied to her!

He could have protected her by telling her Jocelyne was in town instead of distancing himself and lying to her about being busy at work. If she knew that Jocelyne was in Florida, she would have never visited his home. Although by lying to her, she was able to discover the hurtful truths. How dare he lie to her and think she was so superficial that his cards and words could erase his betrayal and lies? He could have also jumped in and be a hero and corrected Jocelyne at that time, but he did not. He just stood there and watched as she was being humiliated and degraded by his wife.

How could he be okay with her being insulted, knowing that she was innocent? For this, she could not forgive him so soon. Orianthi wanted him to suffer as much as she was hurting; she wanted him to understand how his actions and omissions maimed her. She refused to entertain his pointless rationale at this point. She missed him tremendously more than life itself. However, Orianthi wished that she could erase the past two weeks. She wished that she could hear his voice before bed, she would give anything to have his arms around her, but if his arms are not willing to protect her, he should not have the right to love her. He had a million opportunities, to be totally honest with her. All this time with him, Orianthi thought she was building her life with NXavier, and to him she was only his side piece, his mistress, his concubine. How can she ever face him again? NXavier used a subtle way to pull a rug off under her feet and left her sinking in a black hole, alone and deserted.

By the middle of the third week of the breakup, Lianii and Zainii were back home for school, and Orianthi kept herself busy with getting Lianii ready. Thoughts of NXavier haunted her, mostly at nights and when she was alone. She finally wandered into the guest room one day when Lianii asked about the origins of those gifts. Orianthi realized that she had unconsciously suppressed any memory of NXavier's gifts and cards. The flowers were a constant reminder of him, but other trinkets were stacked against a wall appearing as lonely as she felt. Orianthi asked Lianii to assist her in carrying them to her room with her so the gifts would not be too remote. Orianthi had fallen into a pattern at work and at home.

She was a workaholic and pushed her staff to the brink of insanity, they knew that she was dealing with something because she refused the deliveries of her meals at work and gave her daily floral deliveries to a lonely patient. Although she seemed sadder, the staff only wanted to hug her. If free, she would be closed on her computer working. At home she was mechanical; she was always busy with school and had completed most of her coursework ahead of schedule and her other classmates. Lianii was worried about her mom being so quiet, tired, and apart from random hugs to her, and for no reason she stayed busy working on her computer. Lianii knew that her change had something to do with NXavier's disappearance. On the third week of her return, when she could not live with the shell of her mom any longer, she left NXavier a message asking him to please fix her mom because she was not behaving normally.

Lianii texted her aunts and wondered what they could do to cheer up her robotic mother. She needed her sweet, cheerful mom back by any means possible. Lianii was shocked when NXavier suggested a 5-day cruise for her mother and her girlfriend.

Lianii called her aunts and asked them to plan an all-expenses-paid cruise for them courtesy of NXavier and to drag her mom with them. Orianthi had refused all festivities with her girlfriends since that fatal day with Jocelyne. She had conveniently declined to partake in any plans pretending she was swamped. Lianii left NXavier a message regarding the girls' interest in the cruise, although no one knew how to get Orianthi to go. The friends decided to go over to Orianthi for an intervention as a means to guilt her into going on this free cruise.

Orianthi was surprised to see Mia, Lorelei, and Zainii at her door with dinner. She knew that they ambushed her because she would have never approved of this visit. She smiled when she realized her friends knew that she was avoiding them, and they probably had enough of her distancing. They enjoyed the meals in silence until Lianii and Zainii started talking about going five-day trip in October. The girls would be traveling to an Indian reservation for a school project with their school. They sounded quite excited about their cruise. Mia thought this would be the ideal time to go on their cruise. She asked Orianthi and Lorelai to consider going on an all-expense five-day long cruise with her while the girls were on their trips. Lorelai agreed immediately, but it took much more convincing to get Orianthi to decide to tag along.

Once she was on board, Lianii texted NXavier, who instantly secured a suite on the 9th floor on the Norwegian cruise liner. NXavier was happy to be doing something that he knows Orianthi would enjoy. He secured their tickets and would get their itinerary mailed to Mia anonymously. Then he texted Lianii to confirmed it had been taken care of. Lianii confided in Zainii and swore her to secrecy. She needed to have her mom back by any means necessary, and if a paid cruise by NXavier fixed her mom, she would do it every day for a month. The girls were happy with their secret plans and hurried off to Lianii bedroom before they were exposed through their guilt.

A week later, Orianthi sat in her office after a long, frustrating day with never-ending meetings while nursing a throbbing headache. She was exhausted and could hardly wait for this upcoming cruise. She needed some distance from NXavier, a cruise would be perfect. She was counting the seconds before they leave and with her hands cupping her face there was a knock at her door. She beckoned the disturber of her peace in, and without lifting her face out of her hands, she waited for the culprit to talk. No words came out which forced her to lift up her head irritatingly and open her eyes... Standing in her office was the unit secretary too afraid to disturb her and a bashful, freshly- shaved NXavier. He appeared much hotter than before. The sight of him standing so close to her cripples her. Thank God for this solid desk between them. She remained seated, not that her legs could carry her if she were to stand.

Orianthi felt flushed; her heart was pounding, ready to jump out of her chest. She missed NXavier immensely. She felt the pressure increased at the back of her head as she attempted to calm down and thank the Secretary for her efforts, then turned to NXavier as the secretary exited her office.

She refrained from looking at him because she knew if she did she would have him take her right here on the solid desk. He started to apologize for disturbing her at work as she fervently attempted to mute his words in her mind. She was not interested in any of his stories, his reasons, his explanations, or his apologies. She only wanted to get to her home, have a long shower, pop in a few Aleve tablets in her mouth for this excruciating pain, and flush them down with a glass of wine. Orianthi motioned to her head to indicate her pulsating headache and politely inform NXavier that she would not entertain a conversation on any of his preferred issues at her job now or in the future.

She was not ready to talk to him and would inform him of the time and venue for a discussion. Then she kindly asked him to leave. He left her office, and she walked to the door, locked it, and slipped down to the floor in tears. She loved this man, so being so close to him and not running into his arms, kissing him, or massaging his firm arms left her crippled. Orianthi stayed on the floor until she felt strong enough to walk to her sink and washed her face. She prayed that no one needed her until the end of her shift because she needed to regain her composure before she walked out of her office. She made it to her car in the parking lot and found NXavier not only parked near her car but lounging on his vehicle between their cars waiting on her. She attempted to get past him without stopping, and his arm snaked out and wrapped itself around her resisting body.

NXavier pressed her limp body into his chest, oblivious to others seeing them.

She may not want to speak to him, but he knows that her body misses him as much as he did her soft lips and curvaceous body. He saw how breathless she was in her office with a desk between them. He knows his closeness has an impact on her; he had to find a way to where Orianthi cannot escape his grasp to talk to her. Orianthi seemed to have lost a few pounds in the past few weeks, but she was still the sexiest woman he had ever seen. He held her in his arms until all the resistance slipped from her body, and she remained helpless in his arms. His ambush, and being carried in his arms reminded her of their first encounter many moons ago.

How have times changed since their first night?

He kissed her forehead and lightly laid soft kisses on her cheeks until he captured her lips into an earth-shattering kiss. Orianthi did not know how much she misses NXavier until that kiss rebooted her suppressed senses.

Orianthi found out that she needed the kiss more than the oxygen that she breathes, needed to feel NXavier's strong arms around her to be rejuvenated. In spite of the pain coursing through her body, she needed the only person in the world who could heal her. Orianthi allowed his kisses until he sucked the pain out of her body, and she felt strong enough to walk away from his enticing arms. She felt much better than she had felt in weeks. She needed this kiss, she needs him, in spite of the lies, in spite of the betrayal she needed him. She may need to use this remedy to get over him. Occasional doses of him tapered off until she was over him ultimately. Orianthi extracted herself from his powerful grasp, opened her car, and drove off living NXavier standing in the parking lot, wondering what his next move would be.

Chapter 21

UNRELENTING PUNISHMENT

Orianthi pulled onto her street and was surprised to see NXavier's car in her driveway. She was not in the mood to do another car by car groping tonight. She had an insufferable day. Lianii was spending the weekend with Mia since she hosted Zainii last weekend. Orianthi was aching to get home to a hot shower, a quick meal, and her soft bed. She was dreading the upcoming confrontation with NXavier. She wondered if he had any right to demand to spend time with her after all that he put her through. Yes, she misses him, but from now on, she would need to regain control of this ship, which is her life. She had so much to say to him, maybe actually telling him how much he hurt her will give him the ammunition he needs to stay away from her.

She loved him profoundly, and his absences crippled her to her core. Surely he knew that as his new girlfriend, Orianthi had grown to understand her role in his life, but this role was only activated if his family was visiting him in Florida, or while he is in Quebec. She would refrain from calling, sure he was happy with that because it meant his wife would not know of her existence. Right now she feels like a complete fool; how could she have missed those signs. Is she that naive? When Orianthi got to his car it was empty, where could he be?

She texted Mia to confirmed she had Lianii and walked to her door, which was surprisingly unlocked. As she opened the door, she saw NXavier standing next to the island in her kitchen. He turned to face her with a questioning smile on his face, trying to assess her mood. By her puzzled look, NXavier quickly explained that Lianii was home when he knocked, and she let him into the house. He seemed taller tonight, or maybe she was shorter these days. The sight of him always leaves her breathless. He was a very handsome guy who was oblivious to his looks. He had on jeans that fit snugly around his lean hips and a royal blue shirt, open at his chest, which revealed the curly hairs underneath. He had his sleeves rolled up to his elbows and had on his slippers. He seemed quite comfortable in her home. She also sported his laptop nearby, which indicated he was thinking of spending the night.

Did he now? Let us see about that! She thought.

She inhaled deeply to calm her shameless heart, walked through the door, and over to him on the couch. When she got close to him, he planted a soft kiss on his forehead. This was the first time she voluntarily touched him since the encounter with Jocelyne. This was part of her plan to punish him later. His scent mesmerizing her senses; her body was hungry for him. As his hands went up to hold her, she pushed them away and walked passed him and entered her bedroom. NXavier sensed that Orianthi was upset, so he allowed her this first indiscretion. Furthermore, he was walking on thin ice with her, asserting is authority will only anger her. She knew that he may not permit any more of those rebuffs from her, so she would need to play her games right tonight. She feels lost without him and actually hated this unnatural distance between them, but after finding out about his lies, she was not in the mood to indulge his whims tonight. Orianthi was angry and was not ready to forgive him as yet. She had been avoiding his calls for almost two months, which probably prompted his impromptu visit tonight.

Although she misses him tremendously, she needed him to understand that there are repercussions to his actions. She misses his arms around her soft body, his tantalizing kisses around her neck, she misses the way his deep kisses paralyzed her soul, but she needed to prove a point tonight. She may love him with every cell of her being, but she would not be lied to or treated like a doormat. Orianthi knew she had some leverage in this relationship, and although she was only his mistress, yes, she was also a mistress that he loves or loved. Who knows if he really did love her? She disappeared into her bedroom, slipped into a pair of tight, white shorts and an orange tank top and walked back into the kitchen to prepare her dinner. NXavier could eat too, he was hungry, but she was not catering to him. She turned on the music while she worked to avoid a conversation with NXavier and danced while working.

The sound of her favorite French playlist of VAYB, Jade, Phyllissa ♡ Ross, and Gabel could be heard from the kitchen, the same artist from the concert in Martinique. The French songs highlighted the differences between their Martinique vacation and now. He hated her aloof* attitude towards him, but he knew that she was only retaliating because of his lies and absence after Martinique. He came close and leaned on the frame of the kitchen doorway, watching her dance provocatively. She ignored him entirely. She danced to those French songs impeccably! He was immensely bothered by the sight of her curvaceous body, moving rhythmically to the songs. He wished that he was holding and thrusting into her with every twist of her hips right at the sink but thought better of it. He felt a powerful yearning for her, which she would have usually taken care of at this point if she was not upset with him. He knew that she would not let him touch her until he had given an explanation for his many lies.

He knew that Orianthi was hurting, and he wished with all his heart that he could protect her from the pain, but he was unable to shield her from the truth and Jocelyne's wrath. He needed to tell her about his marriage to Jocelyne. He needed to be honest with her and hopes to continue to that he could not promise that he would never hurt her again. He wished that he could promise Orianthi her heart's desires, but with the boys and his wife returning to Florida and back in his life she was the ♡ only part of his life; unfortunately, that could be adjusted. He had not yet disclosed to her that Jocelyne now wanted to live with him and his sons in Florida. Jocelyne felt that being in Florida would give her a better angle to stop NXavier from being close to this 'Orianthi.' He wished he could tell her those words without making her feel insignificant. He could guarantee she would not be happy with this news, so to avoid telling her he stayed away.

He was startled out of his pondering mood by her brushing passing past him in the doorway. She was so close to him that he could smell the coconut-scented shampoo she loves, and a hint of the French Lavender and Honey Bath and Body Work's fragrance that she wore today. She left their meals simmering on a low fire and walked past him in the doorway to their bedroom. He longed to pull her to him but sensed that his arms were still unwelcome. He watched her walk into the room and followed her in there, hoping she was ready to talk. She pulled off her tank top, shorts, and her matching lacey undergarments and stood naked before him. NXavier sat at the edge of the bed eyes staring at her shaven fortress, contemplating on making her his tonight and how much he had missed making love to her.

NXavier felt himself throbbing between the sultry dancing in the kitchen and the sight of her shaven pussy; he was in agony! What was she doing undressing in his presence?

He attempted to engage her; she increased the volume of the music and walked into the shower but left the door open. Orianthi continued to dance at the sink as she brushed her teeth, quite aware that NXavier was able to see her from his location in the bedroom. She finished at the sink, slid the glass shower door, walked in, and started her warm shower. She wet her body slowly, knowing he was watching her. She could feel his eyes on her. She raised one leg to rest on the side of the shower to lather her leg and did the same to lather the next. They usually shower together, and NXavier wondered if he should join her now because they often showered together. NXavier grieved for his previous closeness to Orianthi as he would have had this sweet pleasure lathering her smooth skin in the shower before he bent her over and devoured her.

She turned deliberately away from him to scrub her feet to give him a full view of the wet plum garden through the glass doors. He wished he was standing behind her naked and ready to remind her of his powers over her; instead, he remained paralyzed in the spot at the edge of the bed. Orianthi turned off the water and opened the glass door, giving him a clear glimpse of her glistering wet body before she leisurely wrapped her voluptuous body into a thick yellow towel. She dried herself thoroughly, ensuring that she bent away again to dry her feet and did so excruciatingly slow. His view of her 'snatch' and round firm globes was precisely why she did it. She wanted him tortured, she tried to give him a full look of her clean opening. She walked into the room and lift one leg at the edge of the bed to apply lotion to her thighs and lower legs. From his position next to her, he could see her clit, it appeared moist, and he ached to lick the moisture of her clit. She continued to lotion her thigh in mock obliviousness. From her periphery, she continued to observe the range of emotions on his face to her deliberate actions.

She laid at the foot of the bed away from him and opened her thighs. With one hand, she brought her dark, round nipple to her mouth and succulently suck on the tip, and with her other hand, she petted her freshly, scrubbed epicenter lightly. NXavier stared at her, hoping that she would ask him to join her, but all she did was acknowledge that she was ready to listen to his chosen version of affairs but proceeded to touch her body provocatively and suck on her huge nipples. He was rubbing his now engorged member in anticipation of filling her up, but she reminded him that she was listening. He was distracted, uncomfortable, horny, and confused. How was he supposed to explain his predicament to her when she was obviously punishing him? He started detailing his issues with work but was distracted as she opened her lower lips and gently insert her finger into her pink opening.

She continued to stroke her red folds enticingly until her finger was coated with her juices. NXavier wished he was allowed to replace her fingers with his tongue. He pulled his hard pulsating shaft out of its prison, and it stood erect and menacing. She could observe the moisture at the tip of the dark knob but would not be swayed tonight. She ignored NXavier's beautiful erection and urged him to continue his explanation all the time aching to lower herself onto this hard throbbing member. She longed to feel him fill her up to her throat, but though she loves him, she will not tolerate being taken for granted by him or anyone ever again. He would have never allowed her to get away with her current actions, unless if he is aware that he created this present issue. She reminded him to stay on topic as she pulled her finger out of her slippery crevice and brought the coated finger to her waiting lips. She licked the juices off her fingers and inserted said finger back into her starving folds, ensuring that she kept on staring at his face as she continued her exploration of her swollen lower lips.

He stammered, his gaze darted from her lips to her snatch, he appeared quite bothered. He licked his own lips as she continued to urge him for details of his explanation. She quickened her massage of her clitoral region and continue to suck on her nipples. Her breathing rate increased, breaths became shallow, she felt her first climatic urges deep inside her abdomen. He moaned, she ignored him. She never took her eyes off him through the entire masturbation scene. She then reached over for her purse and pulled out a toy, lubricate it with her tongue and mouth seductively and slowly inserted it into her soft opening a few feet away from his pulsating probe. He stopped what he was saying at the site of her toy, wondering how often she had used this toy?

He looked at her in astonishment, wondering why was she carrying a toy in her bag to work? Does she have any more? Why had she never introduced a toy in their bed with him before today?

NXavier needed answers to all those questions but was too engrossed by the image of the toy in her moistened haven to object at this time. He wished that he could take her over his knee and spank her for her present behavior. One thing he was sure of was that he would address her insolence as soon as his punishment is over, and normalcy had returned in their lives. How long can he allow her to continue with her anger without losing her? What else is she hiding from him? She would pay for her impertinence he would ensure that this scenario never reoccurred. His eyes darted to the beautiful tableau laid out a few feet from him and groaned loudly as she filled her velvety meadow with the hard, pulsating toy until it disappeared inside of her moist crevice. She turned on the toy remotely, her body pulsating in ecstasy. She ground rhythmically to the pulsation of the toy, while he stared at the view before him in amazement.

His sweet, submissive mistress was turning into a firecracker right before his eyes. He wanted to stop her and demand answers to his questions but was too mesmerized by her sultry behavior. His hands grabbed at his throbbing shaft, he could hardly wait to bury it to the hilt inside of her. Orianthi's rhythmic movements intensified until she screamed in agony as an orgasm swept over her. Orianthi remained still until the wave was over, and she limp body laid spent on the bed as her breathing slowly stabilized. She never removed her eyes off his face. She pulled out the toy slowly from her tight garden and brought it to her lips one last time, licking at the juices just for his enjoyment or pain. She then rolled off the opposite side of the bed away from his reach, disappeared into the dark bathroom and lock the door behind her, leaving him alone, massaging his engorged member.

Chapter 22

UNWILLING CLOSURE

Orianthi quickly showered, remembering the dinner simmering on the stove. She slipped into a sheer long white negligee to wear to dinner and walked into the bedroom.

NXavier eyes lit up when he saw what she was wearing. The sheer negligee that she chose left nothing to the imagination, he became instantly engorged again. The nightgown she decided, was all lace, with a built-in bra which accentuates her huge globes perfectly, and huge splits from her waist down both thighs. Orianthi refrained from wearing the matching panties, which came with the negligee. His eyes followed her lustfully as she moved around the room. She glanced at his erected pole, still throbbing in his hand and walked towards him. She saw a fleeting smile crossed his face, a smile that weakened her resolve every time. He had a power over her that made it impossible for her to think straight but not tonight!!! She would not submit to her need for him, not tonight. He would have to leave just the way he came. They will be clearing out all misconceptions tonight, not here to give him any sexual release.

She was resilient tonight, she needed to be. NXavier's punishment needed to continue because he lied to her; he did not trust her with the truth. He did not consider her enough of a partner, or he could have confided wholly in her; instead, he took their love for granted. Surely he needed to pay for the pain that his omissions had caused. She walked over to the bed, leaned directly over his phallus, and opened her soft lips around it. She lowered her head and mouth over him until the tip of the shaft could be felt in her throat in one deep suck. She enjoyed sucking his massive cock. Her pussy ached to feel him buried to the hilt in her. She could taste the pre-cum oozing from his tip. How she loved this dick buried in her. She loved being so close to him, inhaling his musky scent. His lithe body was begging to be straddled and rode upon, but this was not the time for his release, let him suffer for hurting her. He asked her to continue, she felt his hand attempting to hold her head, and she brushed his hands away angrily and stood up, pulling her mouth off his now throbbing shaft. She wiped off her lips, straightened out her negligee, and walked through the door without a backward glance.

He laid there paralyzed and angry, wondering how long she would keep on with this torturing of him? Surely she knew that he loved her, and he only stayed away and stayed quiet to protect her. He never planned to have Jocelyne attack her. He regrets the pain caused to her tremendously.

So why was she so stubborn?

Orianthi must know by now that she means the world to him. How is it so easy to seduce him and halt it off midway? This was a new Orianthi, he had never seen this side of her. He would hate to know that he created this new cruel Orianthi. At first glance of her, he is engorged. He had done everything he could to be with her, to apologize to her, it had been weeks since he made love to her, how could she distance herself from him for so long? NXavier felt a constant pain in his chest where his beating heart used to be from missing her. He missed Orianthi, he missed their comfortable life together. He missed their weekends together. She completes him, how was it possible that she could stay away from him?

NXavier heard Orianthi calling him for dinner, so he got off the bed, composed himself, went to the bathroom to freshen up, and walked out to join Orianthi. The table was exquisitely set, candles everywhere. Maybe his delightful Orianthi was returning to him, he hoped. His favorite meal awaited him. Even when she was upset with him, she cooked his favorite meal. He really loves her, and losing her would be catastrophic. He realized at that precise moment with her sitting across from him at the table, that he needed her in his life. He started by telling her that he was sorry, she did not seem impressed by his apology. For the next 40 minutes he told her the truth about the status of his relationship with Jocelyne. He told her about Jocelyne's admission of not being in love with him which was okay because he was not in love with her as well. How he truly loved her, Orianthi, and has never been intimate with Jocelyne not once since he met her or years before. He responded to all her many questions honestly which made Orianthi question her existence in his life.

She was still quite angry that he was only honest with her now. Orianthi would have preferred this honesty during their relationship, not now. Finally, he then told her about Jocelyne's ultimatums and about the three options she gave him. Why he refused to consider Jocelyne's other two options and chose this option because this was the only option in which he could continue to see her. He misses his boys and would give anything to have his family back home, but he would still like things to remain the same with Orianthi. NXavier went on to say, "Jocelyne is not wrong in her demands, she has had the full responsibility of raising their boys, he could not, in all honesty, deny her the chance to move to Florida with the boys." NXavier ended with "for the sake of the boys he would like to see if there is any chance of reconciliation with Jocelyne."

Orianthi stared down at her fingers for a long time as he spoke, feeling numb with each word. She was used to his stories about his spouse, now she wondered which of his stories were true. She asked if any of his admissions tonight of his relationship were true, why were they subjecting their sons to their endless indecisiveness? She was too numb to cry, NXavier's words stunk to her inner core, she felt like he had thrust his hand down her throat and pulled her heart out of her pleural cavity all over again. He was contemplating going back to Jocelyne, how dare he? What was she? Did she mean anything to him? How much more of this disaster can she take?

Orianthi had given him the benefit of the doubt, she had believed him even after she caught him in a lie about his relationship to Jocelyne, she had loved him unconditionally and trusted him with her life. Now he is expecting her to be the sacrificial lamb while he sees where his relationship lies. NXavier claimed he was divorced when they met, and Orianthi believed him, she thought that she had found her soulmate, she thought

NXavier would propose; instead, he reveals that his family was moving here from Quebec and he was considering reconciliation with his wife.

Orianthi rose from the table without saying a word; he watched her walked around the kitchen, tidying up, as though he had not just destroyed all hopes of being with him. She was done! She could not entertain these absurdities one more day. She fought tears at the prospect of leaving him and missing him. She now realized that she had lost all tolerance for waiting. Waiting for him to be free, waiting for him to be hers, waiting for him to love her enough, and finally waiting for him to choose her. She could not be happy with being his second choice; although she understood his need to be close to his sons, Orianthi would be damn if she allowed him continuous access to her on his dreary days. She remained silent because she doubted the words that would come out had she try to speak. How many failed dates would she have to endure before he was lonely again?? She left him at the table eating as she set about to store the remaining meal in the refrigerator.

He was puzzled at her lack of interest in continuing their relationship; she seemed very cold and distant. This is the one day he wished she was screaming at him in frustration about his decisions. At least if she were crying and screaming he would be able to gauge her level of anger, but her silence was disheartening. She bent over at the refrigerator and pulled open the lowest draw. Her negligee barely covered her round firm butt cheeks, so as she bent away from him, which gave him a clear view of her ample garden through the translucent red lace. She stayed there digging for a while until she came out with a long seedless cucumber. He was happy to see her with it, knowing that she loved cucumber salad. He was delighted that she was finally getting something to eat since she placed her dinner in the fridge.

She walked back and stood at the sink, peeling the thin, long, cucumber while she danced to the Eric Donaldson music playing on her playlist. She had to distract herself somehow instead of redundantly complaining about his decisions. She just could not lose him again. She peeled the cucumber and placed it on a plate. Orianthi could feel his eyes on her every move, and she was counting on just that. She walked over to the leather chaise lounge directly opposite him at the table and sat down. She threw her legs on either side and gave him a full view of her inviting fortress. She then proceeded to open her lips and brought the cold cucumber to her aching clit. She rubbed her clit slowly at first then increased the pace as she saw NXavier licked his lips and swallowed. She loved how the sight of her fat crevice unnerved him. She brought the cucumber to her velvety opening and back up to her clit then brought the cucumber to her mouth as she sucked on it slowly as she did his member earlier.

His appetite for food had vanished at this point as he pushed his meal away to watch her display. She moaned as she brought the cucumber back to her pulsating clit and quivering hole. She rubbed her clit and proceeded to open her lips and push the cucumber into her tightness slowly. Orianthi heard his sharp intake of breath and saw him getting off the table as he walked towards her. He had all he could endure of her games tonight. He was done tolerating her behavior at his expense. It seems she was craving for him to spank her tonight, well a spanking he would provide with pleasure. He expected a candid discussion with her tonight about their love and their future, and all she had done instead was torturing him. Well, she deserved to be placed across his knees at this point. He stood up and pulled her to him roughly. She felt the tension in his muscles as his arms pressed her body to him.

He wanted her to feel his need for her, his agony, his pain. He stared at her lips for a few seconds before he captured her lips in a brutal kiss. Orianthi could no longer hold back her tears as she felt his lips devouring her. How was she going to say goodbye to him at the end of this night? She loved him so much! She continued to cry silently in exasperation. Why did she ever let herself fall for him so hard when she knew that he may leave her eventually? He felt her wet cheeks and paused to lay some soft kisses on her cheeks. He was a powerful man; however, he had a soft side to him that she adored had rarely been seen by others. He was powerless to her tears. Orianthi wished that she could have stayed in his arms forever. She knew that he loved her as much as she loved him. She may need to allow him to leave her to fully commit to his family, but she knew that beyond a doubt, life without him would be unbearable.

After a while, he released her, laid on the chaise lounge, and reached for her again. He suddenly had the urge to taste her juices on his tongue. He positioned her at the head of the chair and reaped the nightgown off her voluptuous body and brought his lips down her inner thigh, and then kissed the other hungrily. She ached to feel his hot lips on her heated mount. She enjoyed his lips on her now; she was sadly looking down at his handiwork. Sad that she loved him so much to sacrifice her love for his family. But she had to stay away from him. She closed her eyes in ecstasy. NXavier alone had the power to melt her; her body only responded in this manner to him. How is she supposed to replace him? The tears stung her closed eyes at the thought of moving on. She jolted when his lips rested on her sore, swollen vaginal lips. He licked and sucked her until her body collapsed over him with the wave of another orgasm. NXavier stood up and walked to the closet and grabbed a thick blanket and some pillows, and made his way to the carpeted floor in front of the electric fireplace.

NXavier opened the blanket and strategically placed the pillows facing the fake flames. He came back for Orianthi's insatiable body and pulled her up to him and captured her lips into a deep passionate kiss. She was pushed up so close to him that she could feel his engorged member pressing into her. He walked her over to the blanket and pillows, once there he started kissing her feverishly, she broke the kiss and dropped to the blankets on the floor, thinking the floor was not the right place for her final night with him. But she craved him so much, she missed his touch the past few weeks, and she desired him so desperately. She would have been with him anywhere once he was willing, but tonight she just wanted intimacy. Deep in thought and concentration, she was surprised when he pulled her to rest on his chest as she then told him how he was free to be with his family. He was shocked by her words. Orianthi told him she would not be waiting on the sideline to see him when he can spare five minutes to see her.

He tried to interject, but she continued with no, no, no! She would not subject herself to more of his excuses, lies, and his pretense. Yes, she loved NXavier, but if he chose to work on his relationship with Jocelyne for the sake of his children, he should do so without having her on the sideline as a distraction. He needed to fully commit to his marriage, and she would have never dated him if she knew he was married." Finally, she said if she could not have all of him, she was not prepared to share him with Jocelyne or anyone. As far as she was concerned he needed to be with his family. After saying those words which shattered NXavier's world to pieces and destroyed all hopes he had for them, she drifted off to a night of deep sleep.

He could not sleep, so he stayed awake staring at her beautiful face hoping by morning she would reconsider. NXavier enjoyed having her to himself, holding her in his arm and kissing her forehead while she slept on his chest.

She was awakened to the sounds of him getting dressed. He seemed lost in thought by her declaration, but she needed him to concentrate on his family and let her go. He did not understand her decision and vehemently opposed her decision. She was adamant that he needed to go away because she could not handle what she went through in the past few weeks. She had to cut him off, she had no choice. Orianthi loved him but was not a homewrecker as much as Jocelyne thought she was. She stared at him, trying to memorize every inch of his firm, muscular body. This was the last time she would be near him. Tears clouded her eyes, and he bent over to kiss her one last time. She wrapped her arms around him as she needed to feel him next to her one last time. He kissed her forehead, bid her goodbye and walked out of the door and out of her life forever. The tears slipped down her cheeks unabashedly.

She wished that she could ask him to stay, hoped that he could have chosen her, wished she could make love to him one last time. How would her heart endure life without him? She remained on the chaise lounge paralyzed with grief. The hot tears streaming down her cheeks reminded her that she was not dreaming. She felt lonely, numb, and dejected. She missed everything about him, every role he played in her life, the way he cared about her, protected her, made her feel safe, their conversations, their fights, his arms, their lovemaking. He knew her needs, she is opinionated and sarcastic nature that most individuals found annoying. But not him, he loved her just the way she was. What would she do now? This was her soulmate, the man of her dreams, how she is supposed to live without him?

Chapter **23**

UNCHARTED WATERS

The smell of the sea breeze pulled Orianthi out of her daydreams as she sat in the uber on the way to the port. Their scheduled cruise was finally here, and she looked forward to the five luxurious days of reading, relaxing, drinking, and dancing with her friends. It was still an effort to pull herself from work, Lianii, and school, but everyone needed a break from the status quo, and so did Orianthi. Her staff was having a potluck in her an absence, and Zainii and Lianii were settled on their compound, grateful for the available Wi-Fi. Orianthi needed the sea breeze for clarity, to regroup and to heal. She needed this cruise to figure out a life without NXavier. How was she supposed to live without NXavier? Just thinking of the concept brought tears to her eyes. She needed to go through checking in and getting into her suite before the tears came back as she was always in tears lately. She wished that she was in a single cabin, alone with her thoughts, alone with her daydreams and alone with her tears. Her friends always understood when she needed to be alone, escaping through one of her Lisa Kleypas' novels. She had brought five of those along with her on the cruise.

Orianthi could not extract NXavier's final conversation out of her head - he was staying away because Jocelyne's three ultimatums were: a divorce, NXavier moving back to Quebec, and quitting his job, or she,

Jocelyne moving to Florida with the boys. NXavier chose the third option because the first two options would impact his sons and seeing Orianthi, respectively. The thought of his wife and kids living in Florida with him floored her. She had to cut him off. She had no option. Although she had been his mistress for all those months, not knowing that he lied to her throughout their relationship, and having his family so close to her left a bitter taste in her mouth.

How can she ever trust him again?

She loved him and wanted to spend the rest of her life with him; however, she was not interested in having any part-time fling when his wife is out of town; she would rather be alone. They were issued the keys to their suite and went in search of their cabins.

She chose the room with a private balcony set out away from the other two bedrooms. Her room had a queen-sized bed, television, recliner, sofa, shower, a door leading to her balcony, and an open window to allow her fresh breeze. She could sleep with her window opened, and she loved that. She freshened up and joined her friends on the deck for cocktails. Amazingly she had a great time catching on her friends' latest adventures. She had been so sad, distant, and melancholy for the past two months that she had missed out on all developments in her friends' lives.

They stayed on deck until it was time for their late- sitting dinner at 8:00 p.m. The women got expertly dressed, each woman a beauty, accomplished, and radiating their confidence. Orianthi looked at herself in the mirror and realized that she had lost a considerable amount of weight in the past few weeks. Orianthi was expected to be there and have fun since she missed a few meals after losing NXavier. Silently she wished everything was back to normal, and NXavier was standing behind her, wrapping his arms around her and kissing her neck.

They had planned on taking a cruise during their relationship, but Martinique came up and so the cruise was postponed. The thought of being here in a suite without NXavier was heartbreaking. The three friends sat to a beautifully prepared seafood dinner in an exquisitely decorated restaurant. Orianthi was thrilled that no one joined them for dinner, which meant they were free to continue with their afternoon conversation.

They chose the fourth chair to secure their bags and enjoyed their meals. For a split second, Orianthi felt an uneasiness up her back, and she was covered with goosebumps. Her friends saw the change in her composure and questioned her. She felt edgy, and it was a feeling like she was being watched or followed. They all turned around and began searching the room but saw no one they recognized. After dinner, Orianthi and her friends returned to their bedroom to change for the night's festivities. She chose a halter top, backless, mid-thigh romper, which NXavier had given her as a gift and forbade her from wearing unless he was present. NXavier was no longer a factor in her life, so tonight, she was asserting her independence and decided to free herself by wearing the provocative outfit that she loves. The romper fitted her like her second skin, and she accessorized with a pair of knee-length gladiator sandals.

Her friends did a double-take when they saw her. "Where are you going dressed like this?" Mia asked. Orianthi smiled and replied, "What happens in Vegas stays in Vegas!"

They all laughed at her comment and left their rooms. The ladies went to karaoke, where they sang three of Destiny's Child's songs – Survivor, Emotions, and Independent woman. By the end of the karaoke session, they were the crowd's favorite. While singing Emotions her voice felt raspy, and she closed her eyes to stop the tears from slipping down her cheeks. Orianthi took a deep breath and felt the uncanny sensation that 'someone was walking on her grave.' They ended the song to a round of applause, after which her friends were wondering whether she was cold as she was covered with goosebumps. She responded in the negative as she did not want to worry them and asked that they could go dancing.

The club was comfortably crowded, every song was a huge crowd pleaser, and they danced until they were patched. Although Orianthi had a grand time, she felt sad that she was dancing without NXavier. The dancing was a bad idea because it made her miss him tremendously. She also could not get the feeling of being watched away from her mind, and she knows if NXavier were around he would have protected her. With all those thoughts going through her mind, she could no longer hold back the tears which came flooding down her eyelids. Thoughts of NXavier were destroying her cruise and her time out with her best friends. There was the best club music ever, she was dressed elegant enough, yet here she was tearfully missing NXavier. She finally decided to head back to her suite.

She told her friends that she was heading in and encouraged them to stay and have fun. They saw the tears and knew that she would rather be alone with her thoughts, so they agreed to stay back. She walked over to her suite, allowing her tears to flow freely.

She vividly remembered the last time she saw NXavier and heard his words about Jocelyne was moving to Florida with his sons.

Yes, she was happy for him to be with his family, but what about her?

What about their love?

Did she mean anything to him?

Was her entire time with him just a façade?

Did he consider her just a placeholder?

Not only did he lie to her for months, he casually informed her that she was no longer essential to him as he had made his decision without consulting her. Why did he come into her life and get her to fall madly in love with him when he knew he was not free to love her?

It had been weeks since the betrayal, when will the pain stop?

Orianthi wished she had obtained answers to her many questions instead of punishing NXavier the last time she was with him. The worst part was that she missed him more than it was humanly possible. Orianthi arrived at the suite, her tears blinding her efforts at opening the door with her key. She knew that it was just the first night, but if she were to remain so wrapped in her grief, it would spoil the girls' trip. At some point, she would need to pull herself together for her friends' sake. They should not have to withstand her pain and rejection.

Orianthi walked into the suite and poured herself some red wine from a bottle chilling in a bucket of ice on the table. She then walked into her room, strip out of her clothes, and sank into the soft, comfortable bed with one of her books. The book was of no help to her tonight as her pain was too potent to allow her to escape into a new book. With no Netflix to resort to, she was forced to revert to memories of NXavier. She laid in bed feeling alone on a ship with thousands of people. The ship rocked gently below her, and suddenly it started to rain. The rain compounded her loneliness, and it caused her to miss NXavier even more. In the distance she could hear the sound of the water splashing around the sides of the ship. The night air was crisp, and it was wet out. She relished the sounds of the raindrops on the balcony; thunder roared in the distance and the occasional lightning, which illuminated the night sky. She ached to feel him next to her and wished he was here. How could she continue to feel like that when he caused her so much pain?

It would have been nice if she could enjoy being with her friends tonight, but she opted to escape into a sultry romance novel in her cabin and the ill-fated love story of Orianthi and NXavier currently trending in her brain consistently.

The sights of many lovely couples strolling on deck, holding hands and stealing kisses depressed her. The endless chatter from her friends earlier, made her crave NXavier even more. How could she feel so much pain and still love him so much? She yearned to hear his calming voice just one more time, and she wondered whether he was enjoying the rain as well. She also asked whether it was flooding where he was. She needed to find a way to stop idolizing him while she nursed the heartache he had created. Orianthi must have dozed off for a second and was suddenly awakened to a sound in the room. She tried to check it out, but she was blindfolded.

She did not put on her night mask before bed because she was reading before. How did it get on her face? She thought. She tried to lift her arms to remove the blindfold, but both of her arms were restrained in handcuffs. She assessed her reach and realized that she could not reach her face. What was happening?

Who was responsible for this?

She recalled placing the "Do Not Disturb" sign on her door when she came in and wondered whether she had mistakenly left her the balcony door unlocked. She stilled herself and became aware that she was completely naked under this soft, down comforter. She adjusted her senses to gather information about her surroundings. In her periphery, she could see that the room was dimly lit. The bed was more extensive than the one in her cabin. She could hear someone moving about in the room. Someone was definitely in here, and it was not her friends. She tried to scream but couldn't because she was gagged. She felt around her for a weapon to use and found nothing. Her cellphone and book were gone, and she had them on a pillow next to her. How much did she drink? Was she drunk when she was moved and not wake up? She could see a silhouette of a figure resting on the dresser but no distinguishing features through her soft mask and smelt the oddly familiar cologne. She cursed herself for allowing her melancholy to separate her from her friends. If only she had stayed with them, she would have been safe.

She pushed herself up on an elbow to get a closer view of the assailant and the room. It was a different room, an unusual and more significant bed. The muffled sound of the television from the neighboring cabin could be heard, the rain continued its downpour, and she was not in her room! She became petrified, her heartbeat accelerated, her breathing increased, and she could not scream. How did she get here? Was she kidnapped?

The intruder straightened himself to his full length and walked towards her. She was frozen in fear, and suddenly all thoughts eluded her. She sat in bed, holding the comforter tightly to her chest. She felt him lower his weight on the bed next to her. The room is still too dark, and her blindfold made it impossible to identify him. She exhaled deeply as he roughly removed the comforter off her naked, cold skin. She laid bare in front of him. How could she be modest now when he most probably carried her naked body to this room?

She did not walk here.

She wondered annoyingly, whom could it be? She tried to relieved the night then remembered the few times that she felt like someone was watching her. The goosebumps returned, the feeling that her grave was being trampled upon was back. His callous hand roughly cupped her left breast; she finally developed the courage to slap his hand away from her chest. He grabbed are arms and pinned them at her side. Was this NXavier? Her kidnapper's scent was so familiar. Could it be?

She whispered his name, hoping he would have confirmed, but the kidnapper remained silent. She wished he would turn on the light, but he did not. She attempted to roll off the bed away from him, but he grabbed her arms to stop her resistance; then he prisoned her body below him as he shortened the reach of her handcuffs hanging from the headboard. She recalled that the headboard in her cabin certainly had no handcuffs. He removed the tape from her lips but pressed his finger on her mouth to silence her, and at that point she attempted to bite his finger as he quickly withdrew his hand. He reached for her nipples and firmly squeezed them between his fingers.

He appeared strong, fearless, and confident. Orianthi felt him lightly petting her skin. The fingers on her skin made her body respond shamelessly to his touch, and how his hand moved over her body felt familiar. How was it possible to respond to his touch so blatantly? What was wrong with her? How dare her body respond so audaciously to this brut? He lowered his naked, hard, body onto hers, and his lips sought her treacherous body. She forced herself to remain still as she refused to give him the satisfaction of responding to his unwanted exploration of her body. Orianthi was in a different realm than her kidnapper, and she wondered how long it would take her friends to realize that she was missing. Her kidnapper realized that she was distracted and proceed to spread her thigh opened, which brought her back into the room. She clamped her legs together to prevent access to her lower lips however her actions did not deter her companion. She felt his weight lifting off the bed and heard him fumbling at the foot of the bed. In a few seconds, she felt her legs being yanked apart as restraints already attached to her ankles were being secured to the foot post of the bed.

He returned to her on the bed and rubbed his fingers lightly on her inner thighs. When his fingers probed her soft lips, he was amazed to find her wet. He lowered his lips to her hardened knob while his fingers explored her soft folds, and his tongue licked her crevice. She melted as his tongue touched her. She knew this feeling, and she had been expertly eaten like this before. As his lips touched her skin she shockingly confirmed that it was her NXavier. It must be him! If only her hands could touch him. His cologne, his touch, his licks were all familiar to her. Orianthi whispered his name, and he moaned but did not answer. Did she conjure up his ghost in her desperate need for him to rescue her? It was not his ghost; it was NXavier, in the flesh, she was probably in his cabin, in his bed, on a rainy night, laying on her naked body. He was her kidnapper! How dare he? She tried to goad him to answer by saying hurtful things to him; however, he read right through it and ignored her. The words emanating from her lips made his exploration of her body even more ruthless. She writhed under him as his finger penetrated her wetness. He then pulled out his finger and probed her with his tongue. She was on a cruise ship, breathless, gagged, helpless, blindfolded, and kidnapped by NXavier! Orianthi's ultimate fantasy was being fulfilled, and she was speechless. How did he know?

How did he get on the ship? How did he get into her cabin? How did he get her here?

Where was she? She had a million questions as usual, but he was not in the mood to talk.

She softly moaned his name as his kisses deepened. He shifted his body, and she felt his lips nibbling on her nipples, her neck, and then he kissed her. His kisses were slow at first but deepened to mirror the ferociousness of his hunger for her. He missed her, and he missed feeling her naked body in his arms. He missed feeling her soft body below him. For a long time, he craved an overdose of Orianthi and was determined to satiate himself before the cruise was over. He released her aching arms, and she quickly slapped him. He stopped her and replaced the handcuffs on her wrist without uttering a word. It was the very first time since the incident with Jocelyne that he had any access to her. At their last meeting at her home, she had tortured him to an inch of his life. It was his turn now! She was still upset with him and refused to allow him to interrupt her vacation with her friends by submitting to him willingly. She was determined not to give him that satisfaction.

She refused to allow him the gratification of allowing his touch to sway her. He knew her body, and her body knew him. She was not about to show any signs of weakness. She was mesmerized by the hand that trailed her shivering skin. Her body craved to be filled by him, she missed the feeling of him deep inside her, but she kept her thoughts to herself. She felt him adjust his position to assess her readiness for him. The fingers which opened her were impatiently gentle. He inserted a long finger into her moist crevice over and over as she tried her best to resist his advances. His kisses deepened, and without further delay, he removed his finger and roughly inserted his engorged shaft into her softness as he silenced her scream with his lips.

Chapter 24

DESPERATE MEASURES

NXavier laid in bed next to a sleeping Orianthi, knowing that it was his last time together with her. He was grateful to be able to pull out his plan so effortlessly. He had no regrets of kidnapping Orianthi, he had to, she left him no choice. He wished he had a choice in the matter but was adamant that she did not want anything to do with NXavier ever again. How could she just cut him off, seduce him and eradicate him from her life as though their love's flames were extinguished? He was desperate to see her, desperate to kiss her, desperate to hold her, desperate to make love to her, and make her stay with him. After their last night together she had written him a very detailed letter explaining her reasons for distancing herself from him. He had read her letter in tears, reading about much he hurt her and how much his actions still pained her. Since the final night at her house, she had taken a significant stake in distancing herself from him. She had her telephone number changed, put her home up for sale and avoided all interactions with him. His gifts of flowers and lunches at work were returned and indicating that she was no longer interested in maintaining a friendship with him.

NXavier had lost all hope of seeing Orianthi again, so when Lianii asked that he fixed her broken mom, he was ecstatic. Immediately he remembered how much she loved a cruise, and his plan came to mind. He would send Orianthi and her friends on a journey, but he would tag and activated his plan. Lately she had gone off the grid completely, no visiting her friends, no nights out, and no socialization. He spoke to her friends occasionally and hated to have caused the distance between them. They, too, were concerned about Orianthi; how could he fix her if she refused to breathe the same air he breathed? He was worried about her and agreed with her friends that sending her on cruise may help. Maybe a cruise would get her out of her safe fortress and give him a chance to convince her to rethink her choices. He was excited to plan the cruise because having her on a cruise ship with him, with no chance of escaping would give him ample access to her. She would have nowhere to run, so it was perfect.

Missing her had converted him into a full-blown stalker. He had watched her at nights at work getting into her car, then followed her home on several occasions just to get a glimpse of her existing car. He would sit in her driveway, wishing he could get inside to lay next to her like he was now, or smell her hair. He missed the scent of her hair. He knew that she would never come to him willingly because she knew his family was moving back to Florida to be with him. She was not interested in being his 'mistress' as she wrote. So desperate times call for desperate measures, he had to kidnap her! He needed a prescribed dose of her, and he was going through withdrawal symptoms without her. He loved her and would move mountains to be with her, just not the mountains she would have preferred. She would have preferred that he turned back time and be honest with her from day one. She would have wanted him to be a single man. He is no single and could not change the fact that he lied to her about his relationship status. He needed to plead with her one more time, so he pounced on the idea of a cruise.

He bought their tickets and secured one for himself. He was very grateful to Lianii, who indirectly assisted in persuading her mom to go on the cruise. For days afterward, he expected Orianthi to change her mind, but no messages came. On the day of the cruise, he came in very early and checked before all of them and left their key cards at the checking counter but kept a copy for himself. He bugged their rooms to follow them around, waiting for a moment when he could activate his plans. He heard when the girls came in, listened to Orianthi's friends' attempts at cheering her up. Orianthi still seemed down but was making a concerted effort to enjoy herself for the sake of her friends. NXavier wished it was just him with her on a private cruise. They did discuss going on a cruise many times before, and he would give anything to turn back the time and have his sweet, submissive, insatiable Orianthi in his arms for the next five days. He needed to see her, he needed to be with her, he had no other option. He followed them to dinner and sat away from them but with a great view of Orianthi. She looked stunning tonight. He fell in love all over again, seeing her in this one-shoulder cocktail attire. She had the knack of choosing dresses that were delicately tailored to fit her curvaceous body.

He wished that he was the one to assist her in getting into her outfit tonight, and wanted to be the one sitting across from her at dinner and permitted to look down her cleavage. The girls were in no hurry to be done with dinner, they seemed happy, he captured Orianthi laughing on a few occasions which left him breathless. He also saw her hugged herself a few times and scanned the room in search of someone and which her friends joined in. He barely escaped before the room got to empty by running out of the restaurant unseen while they were occupied with the waiter ordering dessert. He then waited outside the restaurant to gauge their plans for the night. He followed the girls back to their room and remained as they changed for the night activities. He was able to gather that they would be going to karaoke or a live show then the dance club later. He was curious to see what Orianthi was wearing because of the comments erupting from her friends at her attire. He was shocked to realize it was the little backless number he bought her from France in white linen, which fitted her like a second skin. NXavier brandished an instant erection when he saw her in the outfit.

He jokingly forbade her from wearing it unless he was present to protect her. He was stunned that she would wear it on the ship. Surely wearing it must have brought back vivid memories of the night that followed after she tried it on for him. He observed her from a distance, singing tremendously well, he missed hearing her singing as she performed chores around the house. It was beautiful watching her play and listening to her sing with her friends. NXavier had, on many occasions, heard them sing together before, and the crowd seems quite impressed with them. The last song sounded a bit difficult for Orianthi as she faltered at the end, her friends continued to sing until she regained her composure and completed the song. He knew she was thinking of him and it broke his heart, seeing her in pain. He knew that she was still quite sad about the breakup and wished he could walk up to Orianthi and wrapped his arms around her delectable body. After karaoke, the girls went to the club, and he followed in a distance. At the club he watched as she attempted to maintain a cheerful demeanor but failed miserably. She loves dancing and politely declined to dance with anyone who asked her. He saw her speaking to her friends, then hugged them and walked out of the club and headed to their suite.

He listened as she got in removed her shoes and poured a glass of wine, little did she know he spiked the chilled wine with a dose of melatonin. She was fast asleep within minutes of lying down. NXavier accessed their room, wrapped her in a robe, and carried her to his room, he returned to the room to remove the offending wine, bucket, and bug. He also took her belongings out of the room and brought to his room at the end of ship. He ensured to close her door and place a 'do not disturb' sign on her door or his door and waited for the melatonin to wean out of her sleeping body. NXavier blindfolded Orianthi, placed her wrist in soft restraints and watched her sleep. He was alerted to her arousing by the soft moan coming* from her on the nearby bed and the sound of his name, which she repeatedly called in anguish. She was dreaming of him and being tortured in her sleep. He was tempted to wake her up; he wanted to know how the dream proceeded. He rested on the dresser and waited for her to be fully awake to realize that she was not alone in the room.

She woke up and sat up in bed, realizing that she was not in her cabin, she was blindfolded and tried to pull it off her face to explore the room, but her hands could not reach her face because of wrist restraints. NXavier watched as she felt around the bed, apparently trying to locate her phone. He had removed the phone and placed on the dresser. He made decision to remain quiet until he kisses her and make love to her; hopefully she would realize that it was him. If not, the restraints would stay until she was calm and receptive to his advances. She said his name immediately after the first kiss!! He was elated that she did. He continued to make love to her because in blindfold and restraints because Orianthi had relayed to him that it was a fetish of hers after reading the book "50 Shades of Grey." Being a resistant captive was one of her fetishes and now his so, they would explore this life for the remaining four days on the cruise. NXavier whispered to her softly to distort his voice as he continued to ravish her succulent body.

After the scene, he cleansed her with a moist towel as she dosed off from the remaining melatonin or the orgasm. He left her sleeping and stepped out of his cabin to order room service for breakfast. He texted her friends from her phone and said that she had decided to disembark and took a flight home because staying on would destroy their enjoyment on the cruise. He waited for breakfast to arrive then woke her up to feed her. During breakfast, he explained his rationale for his boorish behavior, answered her many questions, and described the rules and expectations of her captivity. She was not allowed to scream, or her gag would return, if she became difficult at any point, he would spank her until she was raw. She did not want to see him, so she would not be allowed to enjoy him. This was only for his canal needs; she would be spanked with any admission of pleasure. He would remove her blindfold but would re-apply them as he needs are met. For the next four days, she was being transformed into her own '50 Shades of Grey. He would bathe her, dress her up and she was not permitted to exit their room or called anyone; otherwise she would be severely punished. He told her about texting her friends and would keep her restraints on for the duration of the cruise.

After breakfast, he decided to escort her to the spacious shower. NXavier shackled Orianthi's feet, loosely to allow her to walk to the shower and restroom at the edge of the room. Orianthi could feel the droplets of water on her legs as she got closer to the running water he had prepared for her. The water was warm, almost too warm, but he remembered how much she enjoyed the hot water on her skin. NXavier removed Orianthi's handcuffs and then ordered her to get into the shower and assisted her under the flow of water. Her wrists were sore and redden from her restraints. The water caressed her soft, inflamed skin and soothed her aching muscles. He took the head of the shower and sprayed her with the warm water as he used his long fingers to rub her skins. His fingers softly kneading her shoulders. He ordered her to turn to face him and sprayed the water on her bruised nipples from his earlier brutal lovemaking. The warm water stung her nipples that were savagely sucked and bitten by his assault earlier. He fingered each of her nipples between his thumb and forefinger, and she cried out in pain at which point he proceeded to silence her with a savage kiss that bruised her lip. His hands moved to her other nipple, and he squeezed it hard even harder as he brought it to his lips.

He placed both nipples between his lips and nibbled on them tenderly, which was amazingly more pleasurable than his fingers. His fingers trailed to her inner thighs as he ordered her to open her shackled legs as wide as the shackles would allow. He poured some soap on the sponge and proceeded to wash her body with one hand as he used his other fingers to gently explore her hot epicenter. She shivered from his touch, he was extremely gentle compared to the other times his fingers had invaded her earlier. He sprayed the water on her sore folds, rubbed and massage her clitoris and gently insert a finger between the moist lips of her inner fortress. A soft moan escaped her lips, and she felt the spanking before his hands connected to her backside. Her body swayed to him, drunkenly from the spanking. He steadied her and brought her chin up to his for another brutal kiss. Her lips felt bruised and sore from the assault. He roughly released her and allowed the hot water to run down her body. She silently welcomed the soothing water on her aching skin. He soaped her face, neck, chest, stomach, thighs, and legs. Then turned her away from him and proceeded to massage her back and sore buttock.

She shuddered from the feelings of his long fingers on her skin. She wished that she could enjoy his nearness forever. The sensation of having him in a shower with her and the hot water did not only affect her; it drove her insane! She missed him tremendously but distanced herself from him because of his lies, not because she stopped loving him. Knowing that he could not be with her was torture. She was happy he planned this cruise and was silently excited that he had kidnapped her. Why couldn't he let her go to nurse her broken heart? How is she supposed to forget him when he knew her every need and made all her dreams come true? Her treacherous body was responding to his touch brazenly. She jolted in pain as his fingers opened her butt cheeks and washed her slowly, the spray of the water lingered on her raw-spanked cheeks. He kneaded each cheek soothingly as he washed them. She loves to feel his fingers stroking her redden cheeks. She felt him withdraw his hands away from her skin and ordered her to turn around.

She turned to see him removing his clothing. She was shocked to see his engorged member. The sight of his naked body sent thrills up her spine.

Her pussy muscles tightened involuntarily at the thought of yet another intrusion. Surely her captor was satiated. She wished she was allowed to touch his lithe body; she ached to trace the contours of his face. She dreamt of being in his arm, being his forever, but she knew that she was only here until the next few days. Surely he could not be engorged again, but yes, he was as he ordered her to kneel in front of him. She did as she was told with the spray of water over her head he directed his hard rod into her mouth. She held his shaft and softly kissed the tip of his pulsating phallus. With shaking hand, she circled the hard shaft between her soft fingers. He moaned as she softly kissed up and down the hardened shaft. She pulled the foreskin down the length of the shaft and replaced with her warm lips. She put the entire member into her mouth until she felt the tip all the way to the back of her throat. She pulled him out of her mouth, slowly savoring his taste on her lips and her hands on him. These were the only instances when she was allowed to touch him so intimately according to his many rules.

Orianthi pushed him through her lips intended to suck him at her pace, but he held the back of her head and thrust himself roughly into her mouth. He fucked her mouth steadily for an eternity then order her turn around on all fours on the shower floor. Her knees were bruised as she complied with his wishes. He positioned himself behind her and opened her swollen lips and with one thrust, roughly inserted his entire rod deep inside her. She screamed at the pain of his sudden thrust. He spanked her cheeks repeatedly for her lack of control and disobedience. As he thrust in her, He slowly kneaded her sore cheeks intermittently. He opened her cheeks and pressed his thumb on her other opening massaging it. Then he opened her cheeks and insert a finger into her anal sphincter. She painfully began to allow his finger to press inside her forbidden region with each thrust. The double invasion weakened her resistance. With each thrust, she felt him getting more prominent as she got tighter. She felt a climax reaped through her entire body and felt his breathing rate increased. The sensation of his thumb massaging her secret space, and his deep thrusts were heavenly.

She loved the way he filled her, she loved how wet she felt in spite of his torture. She felt the senses reeling from his intrusions. She tightened her vaginal muscles around his massive phallus, which disabled him immensely. Her body screamed for release, and with one final thrust they both collapsed into a heap on the floor in an earth-shattering climax.

After the climax, the showered each other like they did before, then he dried her up and escorted her back to bed and handed her a refreshing drink. He revisited the conversation about their relationship which brought tears to Orianthi's eyes. How could he love her and ask her to share him? She wanted him all to herself, wanted to be his forever but would not fool herself into thinking that he would walk away from his family to her. Orianthi believes that if she decided to stay with him, it would have cheapened her memories of him and she did not want that. She agreed enjoy the next few days submitting to this "50 Shades of Grey" fantasy that he created for them, but going forward, he would prefer to keep her distance and let him be with his family.

The next few days were like her first day, even better. As usual, he thought of everything; he had her toys, massage oils, edible panties, videos, rabbit ears, and magazines. She resigned herself and heard herself agreeing to be his girlfriend, but knowing she would change her mind. They enjoyed their days and nights, loving each other much more than they did before. They explored a world that was available to them and was able to forgive, heal and strengthen each other. Their lives were not the ideal and Orianthi was not looking past the end of the cruise. She thought that if this was going to be her final days with him, she might as well allow him to explore her fetishes and bring her to the brink of ecstasy with each mind-boggling orgasm that they enjoyed.

Chapter **25**

UNFORESEEN REALIZATION

It was six months today, six months since Orianthi decided it was best for them to part ways. Six months of forcing himself to live without her smile, without her voice, without holding her in his arms. He knew that the possibility existed where she would be upset after finding out he lied to her, but NXavier always assumed she loved him enough to be there if he needed her. He needed her, missed her, and he would move mountains to be with her. He had not laid eyes on her in six months. His life was not the same; he dreamt of her; he searched for her in every crowd; he felt like a drowning man clinging to a rotten blade of straw. After the breakup, though amicable, Orianthi thought that the right place was with his sons. She sold her home, moved to another County and she changed her telephone number. She severed all connections to him.

He had driven to her old home many times out of habit and called her numerous times, but he could not reach her. Not being able to reach Orianthi broke his heart over and over. Yes, Jocelyne gave an ultimatum, but if he had to choose, he would have selected co-parenting the children and being married to Orianthi in every scenario. Orianthi thought that his decision would impact his sons, she would have considered this scenario if the boys were older, but they were too young. As a nurse, Orianthi understood the impact of divorce on children and would not wish it on NXavier's sons, so she decided to sever all ties with him immediately. Since the kidnapping, he had monitored her from a distance and decided he returned to Quebec to live with Jocelyne and the boys against his mother's wishes as he could not bear to live within Florida without her. He was still married to Jocelyne; however, they continued to live separate lives and were not on speaking terms.

To this day, he still wonders why Jocelyne gave the ultimatum knowing that she did not wish to be intimate with him. He despised the environment in the home between them, and it was not conducive to the boys. They heard about Orianthi through one of the fights and even asked their dad once if he missed her. He answered honestly and told them that Orianthi no longer wanted to be his friend because he was dishonest to her. He was in such pain without her, he threw himself into work to escape and increased his drinking to numb the pain of losing Orianthi. He also made a substantial investment to benefit her life and education and tried to be the best father he could be under the circumstances. He was due to travel to Florida for the first time since he left and wondered if his life would ever be normal again without her because she took his heart with her when she left.

♡~♡~♡~♡~♡~♡~♡

Jocelyne was happy that all was well again in her world. NXavier was home, where he belonged, they were not getting a divorce, and his love interest had vanished from whence she came. Jocelyne had discovered his fling on their trip to France. She was floored to realize how deeply in love he was with this faceless Orianthi. Did her actions push him into this Orianthi's arms? She selfishly decided that she needed him home, and NXavier was sadly mistaken if he believed that she would sacrifice her life for him and the boys while he got to run off in the sunset with someone else. She was surprised to realize that NXavier would have chosen that girl if he had to. He would have selected Orianthi over her and the boys. No, she would not hear of it, not after all the years she had invested in their marriage and all those sacrifices she had made to maintain their family.

She would not be placed on any sideline for his new wife to decide what she and her children would do or get from NXavier. She refused to allow her sons to be displaced. She recognized that NXavier was lonely, he had lost weight, was moody, and probably hated being in this platonic relationship with her, but that was their life. The boys seemed concerned about their melancholy, workaholic dad who currently resides with them and wishes that their 'fun dad' would return. They missed their fun dad and had voiced their concerns on the subject matter. It had been six months since he broke up with Orianthi; surely, he should be over Orianthi by now. He was scheduled to attend a benefit in Florida for the coming weekend. Maybe she should tag along with him to keep him on a straight and narrow path away from Orianthi, she thought. When he returned to Quebec after his trip, she intended to suggest couples therapy for the two of them.

◇◇◇◇◇◇◇◇

Orianthi woke up feeling drained, but happy for the first time in a very long time. She had been running around, keeping herself busy with school, work, and moving on with her new life, a life without NXavier. She had to put her feelings aside because she was quite busy with a work/school project. The bulk of the work was when her Doctoral thesis, a pilot project she created at school, was chosen to be implemented at her job. She designed a holistic approach to Thoracic Care, which allows families to tune in from home to communicate with their relatives. Her project provided home care feeling for families in emergency care situations post Thoracic surgery. The project provided a live stream to allow absentee family members to feel closer to their loved ones while admitted. The live streams would also limit the number of infections occurring in post thoracic surgical patients, and the constant interruption in care.

The rooms were designed to allow trained personnel to continually be on hand to monitor and answer questions that alleviate the fears and concerns of the family members while keeping the patient safe after thoracic surgeries. The state of the art unit was donated to the facility by a silent benefactor who had everyone wondering whether the benefactor was a past or current patient. That was the least of Orianthi's concern; she was just ecstatic that her study and unit were chosen to carry out her doctoral research, and she was due to graduate in the next two months. She needed this project to be a huge success. Lately with the additional workload she barely had the time to feel sorry for herself or to lecture at the university. She took two semesters off her teaching job to complete her coursework.

Her staff moved to the newly constructed, Thoracic Intensive Care unit at her job two days prior. It was a dream to work there, and it boasted all the latest features in technology, equipment, staff lunchroom with its own cafeteria and chef. Orianthi was given a beautifully designed office as the director with her restroom and two conference rooms. The unit had a private elevator and stairs, a vast family waiting room with recliners to sleep on, showers, barista for fresh coffee, and locker rooms to ensure the safest environment.

Orianthi was grateful for the opportunity, the workload, and the distraction since NXavier.

She had missed him tremendously, so this pilot project had been a great distraction and a pseudo replacement of NXavier if there was ever such a concept.

Over the past few weeks, Orianthi had worked diligently with the administrators, finance department, architects, and builders, combining over every minute detail of the project. Now that the unit is completed, and she could not be happier. Finally, she could breathe, sleep in, and relax at least for a day and enjoy her handiwork. The grand opening and fundraising activity was scheduled for the upcoming weekend, and she was expected to be there. She wished that NXavier was here to accompany her to this momentous occasion. He would have been so proud of her. Lately she refrained from socializing because everything reminded her of him. Orianthi had so much work to do that attending a social event seemed tedious, especially if she had to go alone. She had enlisted Mia and Lorelei to accompany her to the opening that Saturday.

Orianthi stood at the window, staring out, wondering what NXavier was doing at this moment. She had not seen or spoken to him in six months, six days, two hours, and fifteen minutes – oh yes, she kept count of the days down to every minute. So much had happened in the past six months. So much she wished she could share with him. She regretted letting him go knowing what she knows now, but his sons were of the highest priority then. Six months, without NXavier and she had yet learned how to regrouped into normalcy. She hated counting the months, the minutes, the days since her break-up with NXavier; however, he was her constant thought, he still was. How could she not think of him! She vividly recalled everything about him, his smile, his kisses, the feel of his skin on hers. She remembered his hectic schedules, his favorite songs, his words, the way he made her feel, and most of all his lovemaking. Her love for him always haunts her, she needed him now more than ever.

She had moved to a new home closer to work and school, and as she could not bear to be in the house, she regularly shared with him. She moved to a new County to be away from him, changed her phone number, purchased a new car and threw herself into her schoolwork. He moved back to Quebec to be with his family as he could not bear to be in Florida and not see Orianthi, and she wishes that he would come back to her daily. He never did.

Lianii had started advanced classes in high school and was scheduled to fly back home for summer this week with Zainii, living Orianthi all alone throughout the semester. She was off today because she had a doctor's appointment and needed to get the necessities for Lianii's trip. She smiled, thinking of how NXavier would react at the thought of her visiting the doctor. A pity she had to give him up along with her heart.

Saturday morning loomed near, and she hoped that the guests would attend to support the worthy cause. The building was built to specification, but significant fundraising would provide the added cushion required to run her unit efficiently. She went into the banquet hall to ensure that decorators and caterers were adequately situated. Afterward, she returned home for a nap before leaving for the grand opening. The girls came over around noon to prepare for the evening, and she was awakening to the sounds of hairstylist and make-up artist working on her friends in preparation for the function. She wished NXavier was there to escort her to tonight's proceeding. For the special evening, she selected a sweetheart sequined spaghetti straps, deep V-Neck, flowy bottom, and cascading trail dress. Her hair and makeup were done impeccably, and she looked exquisite. Her friends dressed in similar outfits and the trio left to enjoy the festivities of the night.

The room was expertly decorated, and there were images of the different areas of the unit framing the walls. Everyone seemed happy to see each other, and anxiously waited to see the amount raised for the evening. They were ushered to their table at the front of the stage, close to the steps because Orianthi did not want to walk too far when her turn came to address the crowd. Orianthi felt tense as she detested public speaking. She was chosen to unveil the name of the unit on stage and had prepared a short speech. No one knew the name chosen for the unit as the silent benefactor decided it. All the staff were eager to see the name and would only be revealed by her tonight. She wished that she could forgo getting up on there.

Since it was her research, she was assigned to introduce her project. Orianthi wished she could sip wine as she always felt more confident after just one sip, but her girlfriends helped calm her nerves by engaging her in conversation. She stilled herself by taking some deep breaths and then reminded herself that this was for school.

Everyone expected the silent benefactor to be introduced, but he was never called.

The festivities went on without any complications; dinner was delicious; they raised $500,000.00 for the unit; it was her time to get up there. Orianthi was assisted up the steps and stood behind the podium, facing the crowd. At first, Orianthi maintained eye contact with Mia and Lorelei for support, but after a few minutes, she started scanning the crowd.

She began with the slide show giving the crowd a digital tour of the unit. She then detailed the goals of the unit, her plans for implementation, and thanked the donors.

As she described her project and goals for the unit, she became quite animated. The crowd was very receptive to her plans and cheered her on and asked numerous questions. Her nervousness left her as she became engrossed in talking about her project. It became time for the grand reveal, so Orianthi walked over to the table to retrieve the envelope. She opened the envelope in full view of the crowd. The unit would be named The Stevens-Dimitri Thoracic Care Unit, hers, and NXavier's last names. He was the silent benefactor! He chose her project; he never left. Tears filled Orianthi's eyes, she suddenly felt dizzy, and the tears rolled down her cheeks. She looked up to search the crowd because she felt strange; this felt so uncanny. She was reminded of the incident on the cruise, and she could feel his presence; NXavier was here. She felt a sudden heat overcome her, and the color drained from her face as her eyes locked with a shocked NXavier staring at her six-month pregnant abdomen from the doorway. He was staring at her with a murderous look that she knew too well. Orianthi looked at her friends in a state of panic, whispered NXavier's name before collapsing with a loud thud on the stage.

About the Author

Lanae Gee is a Nursing Professor by day and a blogger on weekends who lives in South Florida but originated from the exotic Caribbean island of St Lucia. She enjoys expressing herself through writing, teaching, traveling, a cruise, and reading. Lanae Gee loves to read and is greatly influence by Jackie Collins, Danielle Steele, Sidney Sheldon, but prefers to escape in the historical romances of Julia Quinn and Lisa Kleypas. Lanae Gee is a single parent of a son, daughter, and granddaughter. She obtained a nursing degree from Sir Arthur Lewis Community College in St Lucia. Bachelor's and Master's Degrees in nursing and Nursing Education from the University of Phoenix and a Doctorate from Barry University. As the author of "Forbidden Encounters," she is embarking into a new world, onto new dreams, new goals; she hopes that the readers enjoy reading this novel as much as she enjoys writing it.

CPSIA information can be obtained
at www.ICGtesting.com
Printed in the USA
LVHW031656090320
649444LV00002B/326

9 781728 335810